AQUA CR

Part Three

Forever Crystal

by James David

Illustrated by Rex Aldred and James David

First Published in the United Kingdom in 2005
by Moonbeam Publishing
Reprinted 2006

ISBN No. 0-9547704-2-0
EAN No. 978-0954 770426

Bibliographical Data Services
British Library Cataloguing-in-Publication Data
A catalogue record for this book is available
from the British Library

Printed and bound by:
The Max Design & Print Co
Kettlestring Lane, Clifton Moor,
York YO30 4XF

AQUA CRYSTA

Part 1   *Next to No Time*

Part 2   *Deeper Than Yesterday*

Part 3   *Forever Crystal*

Part 4   *StoneSpell*

To
Sadie,
a very special dog we fostered and nursed
for Whitby Dog Rescue until she vanished
and was lost on the Moors.
After eleven days of searching, I found her....
and she then lived a wonderful life with her new owners.
Magic!!

AQUA CRYSTA

Part 3

Forever Crystal

Chapter 1

Something...

    ...somewhere...

        ...wasn't *quite* right.

Something was wrong...

      ...out of place...

        ...amiss.

Something had been lost.

Something that could never *ever* be found again or even replaced.

      The whole forest had sensed it, but the part that noticed it most was the ancient broadleaf copse that crowned *Old Soulsyke's* little hill. The hill that lay more or less in the middle of the great expanse of uniform ranks of evergreens, like a lush island set within an endless ocean.

      For minutes on end, the tiny patch of timeless oaks, beeches and walnuts had fallen silent. Bird song had ceased, and beneath the heavy silence, hosts of flowers had bowed their colourful heads away from the glaring sun. Winged busy, buzzing insects had come to rest. Squirrels stopped their never-ending foraging and even unfurling Springtime ferns had paused and recoiled as if suddenly stung by a Winter's chill.

But, the day was hot...fiercely hot, *baking hot*!... especially for the last day of April...a Friday.

'More like a *'fry-day'*!' thought Jessica to herself, as her fingers delicately fashioned the beginnings of a daisy chain, at the very same moment as her favourite, magical patch of woodland fell silent. She was

miles away, of course, sitting cross-legged on the school grass, half listening to Miss Penny recounting the story of The Great Fire of London. The heat of the afternoon somehow matching the lesson!

It had been even hotter and more uncomfortable indoors, so Miss Penny had decided to take the history lesson outside. All of her pupils in the top class had trooped across the scorching tarmac playground and sat in the shade of the school's old larch tree, either on the grass or on the wooden tree-bench. The tall conifer offered little shelter from the Sun, but it was Jessica's second favourite place in the Upper World. It reminded her of the nearby forest and the magic she and her younger brother had encountered there since they had moved to the North Yorkshire Moors the Summer before.

Just as Miss Penny mentioned the fleeing survivors of the fiery events of 1666, Jessica's mind wandered uncontrollably underground, to the conversation she'd had with Mayor Merrick of Pillo, the eldest inhabitant of *Aqua Crysta*. The snowy haired old man, born a decade before the Great Fire, was approaching his three-hundred and fiftieth year, in Upper World time. It had been amazing for Jessica and Jamie to hear his tale of the Fire and his family's long trek to Northern England. How his mother and father had died and left him and his two sisters with the nasty 'Master of Soulsyke' three centuries before the pine forest had been planted...and how he'd

2

discovered the secret well with its secret cellar...and how, after his sisters had died, he had climbed down the full depth of the well and found the timeless, shrunken world of the 'Crystal Waters' or *Aqua Crysta*...

Jessica suddenly felt a twinge round her neck, a sort of prickling sensation. Her fingers dropped the daisy chain and quickly, again almost uncontrollably, she gently touched the glinting silver charms of her necklace. They seemed to tingle with a fizz of energy. The tiny goblet, the hunting horn and the three miniature woven baskets she had threaded onto the chain last Summer, all glinted and sparkled in the sunlight. Each fizzled as she touched them with her fingertips. But it was the sensation she felt on her skin that surprised her most. It was like nettle stings, but not nettle stings that go on and on, but strange short, sharp ones.

"Jessica Dawson! Are you completely with us!" Miss Penny suddenly enquired, with her hand shielding her eyes from the sun. "Perhaps you'd like to tell the rest of us what you're thinking about! You seem to be miles away!"

"Centuries away, Miss!" replied Jessica dreamily, as though abruptly awakened. "I was just talking to a boy walking by a horse and cart as he and the rest of his family were leaving the flames and smoke of a distant London...!"

At that moment the nettles stopped stinging and Jessica jolted back to the school grass and her fingers carried on weaving the daisy chain. The village clock struck three and, at the very same time, only miles away, the birds started singing again in *Old Soulsyke Wood*. The flowers lifted their heads, the bees began buzzing, the squirrels sprung into life and the green ferns uncoiled.

3

Miss Penny, sympathetic to Jessica's love of history and her vivid imagination, smiled, but at the same time suggested that perhaps the sun was a little too hot, and that the lesson ought to continue back in the classroom.

"Not that we've got a lot of time left!" she continued, as she picked up her handbag. "There's only half-an-hour left before the end of the day...and the long weekend holiday!"

So, with a burble of excited chattering, the top class crocodiled from the grass, across the shimmering tarmac, through the blue doors and into school. And, like her classmates, Jessica's mind was now full of the three days away from school...at *Deer Leap* cottage on the edge of the pine forest...at home with her dad and Jamie. Although, as she tidied her desk, with five minutes to go before half-past three, she couldn't help thinking about the strange sensation she had felt from her necklace and the pictures that had flowed so vividly through her mind. Little did she know that *Aqua Crysta's* magic, once more, was trickling from its secret depths, and that the long weekend ahead was not going to be any old long weekend!

Far from it!

It was going to be a very special weekend.

A *very special* one, indeed!

Of course, back in the broadleaf copse it was of little consequence that the village clock had just struck three. There, time in terms of minutes and hours didn't matter. It was more a matter of season. And on that particular last day of April, although it was supposed to be

Spring, it definitely felt more like Summer!

"I can't believe how hot it is, Jamie!" said Mr Dawson, wiping the sweat from his forehead with his bare arm, as the Land Rover bounced along one of the forest tracks.

"And it's not even mid-day! It's five to three!" gasped his son, who was being thrown all over the place in the passenger seat. "I can't wait to get back to *Deer Leap* for an ice cold drink!"

"I'm afraid you'll have to hang on, son!" said Mr Dawson. "Remember we've got to pick up Jess from school and it's at least a thirty minute drive from here!"

Jessica and Jamies' dad was the Forest Manager. He'd been appointed to the job the Summer before, after nearly ten years as manager of a huge forest in Scotland - the *Queen Mary*. The job had come with a cottage on the edge of the mainly spruce and larch plantation in the middle of the moorlands of North Yorkshire, fairly near the sea. His children had spent their whole lives exploring the '*Mary*', as they'd called the Scottish forest, but now they were getting to know the secrets of '*George*'...the name they'd given to their new forest.

"I bet she's been boiling in school today!" laughed Jamie, as they slowed down at a crossroads of forest tracks.

"Now, now, Jamie," said Mr Dawson, "if I'd known you were going to recover so quickly from your bad stomach, you would have been in school today as well!"

During the previous night Jamie had been quite ill, so his father had decided to keep him at home for the day. But by lunch time he'd perked up, so, as a treat, Jamie had accompanied his dad on an inspection of a stand of larch trees on the far side of the forest.

"Count yourself lucky, I say!" laughed Mr Dawson, as he picked up speed. "Not only have you had an extra day's holiday, but it's your big day tomorrow, too! Luck of the Irish, I say!"

"But, I'm not Irish, I'm Engli..!"

Suddenly, Jamie's father slammed on the brakes. The Land Rover skidded to a halt on the rough track amid a cloud of yellow dust.

"Did you see that? I can't believe it!" exclaimed Mr Dawson, quickly opening his door and jumping onto the track. He leaned back into the Land Rover and grabbed his binoculars off the top of the dashboard.

He then gazed through them intently.
He seemed to be looking at a large bush of dazzlingly bright, golden gorse, one of several that lined the track, separating the glaring roadstone from the tall, dark rows of spruce trees.
As he stared, his mouth fell open in astonishment.

"I've...never!" he gasped in an excited whisper. "I've...never...seen... anything like it...in...my...entire...! Here, son...take a look at that!"
He passed the binoculars to Jamie, at the same time switching off the engine.
Jamie leaned out of his window and focused on the brilliant bush.
"Just to the left of that tall, straggily clump in the middle," his dad whispered. "It's a *nightingale* and it's *with a jay!*"
The two birds had flown across the track and perched together on the gorse bush. The nightingale, not much larger than a robin, but light brown on top and creamy white underneath was dwarfed by the magpie-sized jay. The larger bird's pink chest shone in the sunlight along with its iridescent blue wing streaks.
Its headcrest was brushed up perkily.
"Nightingales are hardly ever seen!" whispered Mr Dawson, his dark bearded face smiling with enthusiasm mixed with wonder,
"and certainly not this far north! And to see one just sitting there with another species is *unbelievable!*"
The two birds sat quite still as their two watchers held their breaths.
"And it's so quiet!" Jamie whispered, gazing through the binoculars.
It was true, the forest was absolutely silent.
There wasn't a sound to be heard.
Mr Dawson glanced at his watch thinking about the journey into the village.
It was two minutes to three.
Suddenly the silence was broken!

A sound, so magnificent and so loud, burst into the air. Its clarity and purity silhouetted against the silence. The whole forest must have heard it! It was the beautiful song of the nightingale!

Jamie lowered his binoculars and listened.

It started with a volley of rapid '*tuk, tuk, weets*' followed by another and another. Then came a slow, haunting melody of single notes of such passion and feeling, hardly believable from such a small creature. Louder and louder, the notes pierced the air, almost in some sort of exclamation of a message, of news. It was as though, the bird was addressing the whole, eerily silent forest and every other living thing was intently listening!

For a full minute the little nightingale heralded its tidings, its song reaching a resounding, mellifluous crescendo...and then...as suddenly as it had begun...it stopped.

For a moment, complete and total silence returned...and then, the forest exploded into birdsong from what seemed like every tree. It was as if a hidden conductor had signalled in the full orchestra after an opening solo. The sound was tremendous, music filling the stifling air. Birds of every kind took to the sky above the tree tops. A certain normality had resumed and even a couple of grey squirrels darted across the track in the distance, each pausing halfway to glance at the Land Rover and its two stunned humans.

Then, as Jamie lifted the binoculars to his eyes, the most amazing thing of all happened!

The jay, a silent spectator throughout the whole of the nightingale's performance, incredibly plucked one of its small, pearly blue wing feathers and presented it, like a bouquet of flowers, to the soloist.

The nightingale took it in its beak, and an instant later, they had both taken to the air and vanished.

The magic was over.

It was one minute past three.

Jamie leaned slowly back in his seat, and his father climbed up beside him. Both were speechless. Mere words couldn't in

7

any way be found to describe what they had just witnessed, but unknown to his father, Jamie had sensed some secret, mystical significance in what he had seen...and, in what he had heard!

There *had* been a message in the song of the nightingale!

Of its meaning he had no notion, but as with his sister, at exactly the same time, he had felt touched by a magic that could only have been woven in one place...a place not too far away, and a place that, once again, was weaving a powerful spell.

A very powerful spell!

Chapter 2

"See you on Tuesday!" called Chloe Biggins as her mum's car pulled away from the pavement outside the village school.

"Have a good holiday!" replied Jessica rather vacantly. She waved a drowsy wave and then returned to the peacock butterfly she was watching on a dandelion sprouting from under the school wall.

As it slowly opened and closed its multi-coloured wings, it reminded her of her favourite picture book when she had just started school. She loved the vivid middle pages showing a woodland view with every possible animal you could imagine. She remembered sitting on a rug in front of the fire in the cottage in Scotland, opening and closing the book and trying to memorise the names of all the animals and birds her mother had taught her. It was a beautiful picture, and even now, seven years later, if she wanted to hear her mother's voice she would just open the middle pages of the book and listen to her naming all the creatures, trees and flowers. It was her mother...Ruth...who had given her a love of nature, and it had been a desperately sad day when she had died from a long illness. The walks in the *Mary* had been wonderful with the mountain paths and waterfalls, the red deer and the golden eagles. The picnics, the Autumn colours, the orphaned fawns they looked after together. If only she was still alive today.

The butterfly suddenly fluttered away. Jessica looked around and realised that everyone had gone home. Where was dad? He was normally there waiting. Always. He never missed. Every school day parked in the lane...generally singing away to himself or clicking his fingers to some 1960s pop tape on the cassette player.

Something must have happened, thought Jessica to herself. Perhaps Jamie's stomach had got worse. Perhaps he'd been rushed to the hospital in Whitby!

Perhaps...

But just as her imagination was about to take off into one of its flights of fancy, she heard a familiar hoot and looked along the lane.

Dad! At last! And besides him, Jamie waving wildly through the open window with his ginger hair blowing all over the place and a broad grin on his freckily face.

"...and then as I was looking at it through dad's binocs, it started singing!" enthused Jamie, as the Land Rover turned onto the main road through the village.

"Its song was terrific!" joined in Mr Dawson. "And to actually see and hear one so close, during the day, and this far north, was pure magic!"

At the word 'magic', Jessica's eyes met Jamie's.

And then when their dad went on about the jay giving the nightingale one of its blue wing feathers, both children knew exactly what the other was thinking!

The blue jay wing feather, the much esteemed and prized treasure of the Aqua Crystans as a bringer of good fortune.

Jamie's bubbling account of the afternoon suddenly stopped, as his mind sank below *George's* deepest roots into the crystal cavern of the secret world...the world of the River Floss, the towns of Galdo and Pillo, and the golden sailing ship called the *Goldcrest*.

At the same time, Jessica imagined the elegant Queen Venetia, and their good friends Lepho and Jonathan and Jane. She thought of the *Palace of Dancing Horses*, the dolls' house, the *Larder Caves*, and the *Cave of Torrents*. She saw *Torrent Lodge* festooned with hundreds of flags with the Magwitch family waving their goodbyes after their last adventure. She saw the sad figure of the Gargoyle she had called Dodo disappearing from view among the stalagmites of the *Star Cavern*... the last time she had seen him...

Suddenly, they were both snapped out of their wonderful, magical memories by the voice of their exuberant father who, of course, was completely unaware of their secrets.

"I think it calls for a double celebration!" he beamed, thudding his hand on the steering wheel.

The children looked into his sparkly blue eyes, wondering what was coming next.

"To mark the splendid happenings in the forest this afternoon and Jamie's tenth birthday tomorrow, I think we ought to drive into Whitby, pick up some fish and chips and have 'em by the sea! How about that, kids?"

"And cokes all round!" burst Jamie.

"And ice creams for seconds!" threw in Jessica for good measure.

"Right, that's a deal!" grinned their dad. "Whitby, here we come!!"

Half-an-hour later they were queueing in their favourite fish and chip shop, Jamie making horrific faces in the shiny, silver metal panels below a hot glass cabinet full of mountains of golden, battered chunks of cod.

"Open or wrapped, sir?" asked the hot faced girl behind the counter.

"Wrapped, please," replied Mr Dawson, as he quickly sprinkled vinegar and salt on the scrumptious, mouth-watering delicacies, before they were quickly bundled into three newspaper parcels.

"Oh, and three chilled cokes, please!" he added, after Jamie had pointed to the tall fridge at the back of the shop and completed his impression of someone dying of thirst in a scorching desert!

After walking along the quayside between the amusement arcades and the bobbing fishing boats, they climbed back into the Land Rover and then drove up the winding road towards Captain Cook's statue. With it being the start of a holiday weekend there were plenty of people about, many of them admiring the view from the cliff top over the harbour to the ruined Abbey and little St. Mary's Church perched on the very edge of East Cliff.

Every time Jessica and Jamie had seen the Abbey since Christmas, they'd thought of the ferocious flames and black smoke they'd watched filling the sky back in the sixteenth century when the enormous, glorious Abbey had been ransacked by King Henry's men. And, how they'd met the fleeing monk, Leonardo, as he was being hounded across the beach by three of the King's men on horseback.

It only seemed like yesterday, but it had happened around four and a half centuries ago! And they had been there to witness it! All because of the time-tunnel built by the Gargoyles in the seacave! It all seemed so incredible!

If their father had known what was going through their minds as he drove along the coast road to Sandsend, the shock surely would have made him drive off the road and into the sea! In fact, he nearly did when Jessica suddenly asked out of the blue,

"Did the roof ever collapse in the cave at Sandsend, Dad?"

"Good gracious, child! How the dickens do you know about that?" he gasped in amazement as the Land Rover momentarily swerved across to the other side of the road.

Mr Dawson, of course, had been puzzled and mystified by one or two strange events since he and his children had moved to *Deer Leap*! Most perplexing of all had been when he'd met Jamie's 'new friend', Jonathan, in the woodland at *Old Soulsyke* the Summer before. The boy had looked exactly like a Jonathan he'd known in the 1950s when he and his parents used to come to Sandsend for their annual July holiday. The boy he'd met in the woods had been his old friend's absolute double! He'd even been dressed like his mate from the 'fifties!

Then at Christmas he'd been truly gobsmacked when he'd opened a mysterious gift from under the Christmas tree! Inside a crumpled brown paper bag he'd found two *Matchbox* toys he vaguely remembered losing at Sandsend railway station fifty years ago! Still in their boxes, in brand new condition, with the message "To Ted, Lost and Found, July 1st 1954" scribbled on the paper bag! It had been a total mystery! And one that still gave him goosebumps every time he thought about it!

"Oh, I... I... read about it somewhere!" mumbled Jessica, after receiving a sharp nudge from Jamie's elbow. "It was in a book at the library about the history of the Yorkshire coast."

"Well, to answer your question," said Mr Dawson, as calmly as he could, "the cave roof *did* collapse a day or two after some amazing fuss had occurred on the beach, one Summer. I can't remember what it was all about now...something about a ridiculous visitor from outer space!"

"You mean an alien landed at *Sandsend*?" gasped Jamie, as his father pulled over to park alongside the beach.

"To be honest, it was a lot of fuss about nothing!" said Mr Dawson, smiling.

"I reckon it was someone dressed up just to spook the holiday makers! I missed all the commotion anyway, because I was in Whitby or something. It was *fifty* years ago, you know? It's all a bit vague. But I *do* remember the cave roof collapsing. It meant that me and m' holiday mates could never go exploring in the old sea-cave again. I must have been about ten years old then. Same age as you, son, tomorrow! Speaking of which, I think we'd better get our choppers round this lot before it all gets cold!"

They clambered out of the Land Rover and sat on a bench overlooking the wide beach and the sea. Unwrapping her newspaper parcel, Jessica couldn't help seeing Leonardo, the monk, desperately running across the sands being chased by the men on horseback, their swords drawn.

13

Jamie, at the same time, pictured the Gargoyles fighting them off, rescuing the monk and then taking his salvaged gold coronet from the Abbey into the sea-cave. He could almost hear the Gargoyles jabbering away in their own strange language as they dragged the cart across the sands.

"I'll tell you another thing I remember as well!" said Mr Dawson, when he'd swallowed his first piece of delicious cod and had a swig of coke. He gazed along the coast to the cliffs of Sandsend, becoming lost in his own memories.

"I remember all the kids kept finding strange greeny white crystals all over the beach for ages after the roof collapse.We used to collect them. We all reckoned the rockfall had destroyed a vein of minerals and the sea had washed all the crystals out of the cave. You know, I bet I've still got one of those crystals back home! I'll try and find it for you."

Jessica and Jamie shovelled golden chip after golden chip into their mouths as their father spoke, both very well aware of the origins of the crystals. They dared a glance at one another with raised, knowing eyebrows, but said nothing.

They had become used to keeping their secrets safe, and Jessica pictured her own greeny white piece of crystal she'd picked up when she and Jamie had helped dismantle the time-tunnel. It was hidden in her bedside drawer. She looked at it almost every night and thought of her befriended, abandoned Gargoyle, Dodo...and pictured him still wandering through the rocky passages way beneath *Aqua Crysta*, with the amazing crystalid creatures buzzing around his fearsome head.

After every single morsel of batter had disappeared, and every drop of coke had been drained, Jessica suggested that they walk along the beach to Sandsend and have an ice-cream each from the little cafe. Nobody argued with the idea so they scrambled down to the beach and strolled along the shore towards the cliffs that ended the couple of miles of sand and pebbles that stretched from Whitby.

"So that's why it's called Sands-*end*!" chirped Jamie, as he tossed a pebble into the sea.

"Of course it is, mastermind!" laughed Jessica, taking off her socks and trainers so she could walk through the gently lapping wavelets.

Soon, they arrived at the village with its little, red roofed houses and guest houses wedged between the sea and a tree covered hillside. The great wood and iron railway viaduct had long since been demolished following the closure of the line along the coast, but the brick station still remained. It was the last building in the village with its grey slate roof and tall chimney stacks. Now it was just a house, but Jessica and Jamie imagined all the happenings of July 1st. 1954 when they'd chased Dodo up from the packed holiday beach onto the viaduct. They imagined the prim railway station suddenly plunged into chaos, the bewildered station-master and the smart camping coach where the young Ted Dawson - their father - had taken them to escape the newspaper reporter. It had been an incredible time!

As they wandered slowly back along the beach, licking their ice-creams, the sun began to slide behind the hill.

"Dad," asked Jessica, "on the way back home, can you show me where you saw the nightingale and the jay? Just in case they're still around. I'd love to see the nightingale especially."

"It's a bit of a long shot, but we'll give it a go!" said Mr Dawson, licking dribbling ice-cream from his cone. "But first we've got to do some shopping at the supermarket in town."

So, after a quick pebble throwing competition, which Mr Dawson won hands down, they all scrambled back into the Land Rover and headed into Whitby.

An hour or so later, the shopping done, they were heading over the moors towards the great expanse of *George*. By now it was just gone eight o'clock, the sun had all but disappeared, and the twilight time had crept stealthily upon them.

With headlight beams bouncing before it, the vehicle trundled along the narrow moorland lanes until it reached the five-barred gate at the start of one of the main forest tracks.

"That's funny," remarked Mr Dawson curiously, "I'm sure we closed the gate when we left the forest this afternoon!"

"We did, dad!" said Jamie. "I'm sure we did!"

The Land Rover turned onto the track and Jessica quickly jumped out and closed the gate behind them.

Darkness was falling rapidly and although it was certainly a lot cooler than it had been five hours earlier, the air still felt warm.

"I reckon we're in for a storm tonight!" said Mr Dawson, as they turned off the main track onto a narrower one. The headlight beams were now much brighter and lit up the gleaming, golden gorse bushes and the tall spruce trees that towered behind them.

Just then, Mr Dawson had one of his 'great ideas'!

"You remember, son, when Jess had *her* tenth birthday in Scotland, and I let her have a go at driving on one of *Mary's* tracks?"

Jamie's eyes nearly lit up as brightly as the headlamps.

"You mean I can have a go...now...tonight...in the dark?"

"Yep, if you *want* to, that is!"

"*Want to*? You bet!" exclaimed Jamie, almost bursting with excitement.

His dad stopped, and while he and Jamie swapped seats,

Jessica listened and watched for any signs of the nightingale.

"They *do* sing at night, don't they?" she asked, poking her head out of the window.

"They do," said her father, also looking ahead into the gorse bushes.

"It was just a bit further along here where we saw it."

Jamie grabbed the steering wheel tightly with both hands, and, with his heart in his mouth, gingerly stretched his right foot down gently onto the accelerator pedal.

With a little jerk, they nudged forward.

"Now keep her nice and steady and no faster," warned Mr Dawson, with his hand hovering over the handbrake in case his son suddenly felt like being a rally driver!

Jamie nodded, and, at no more than walking pace, it crept along the rough, narrow track. His eyes were glued to its yellowy, grit surface, as he gradually became more confident, and, with no trouble at all, he rounded the first bend.

The way ahead was almost dead straight with a slight uphill slope.

"Alright, press the accelerator very, very gently," said Mr Dawson.

"And remember you're not in a Grand Prix!" joked Jessica.

Jamie's toe pressed the pedal and the Land Rover jolted forward at marching speed, the young driver casually leaning his elbow on the open window sill, with the air of an old, expert hand. For a moment he even dared a glance at the bushes in case he caught sight of the nightingale.

Everything was going very well.

There didn't seem to be much at all to this driving business!

But then...it happened!

Without any warning, Jessica suddenly pointed into the bushes ahead and exclaimed,

"There, there it is!"

Jamie, in his excitement, leaned forward, pressed the accelerator a little too hard, and the Land Rover stung into action sending everyone crashing back in their seats.

Mr Dawson, quickly yanked up the handbrake, and the vehicle skidded to a halt, throwing everyone forward this time!

"Phew!" gasped Jamie, his head resting on the steering wheel.
"What happened?"
"And it wasn't even the nightingale!" sighed Jessica. "It was a bat!"
Mr Dawson shook his head and smiled.
"I think I'll take the wheel for the rest of the journey! My nerves can't...!"
He stopped abruptly.

From out of nowhere, all three of their faces suddenly became bathed in a white, dazzlingly glaring light, so bright that each of them instinctively shielded their eyes with their arms.

Two enormous brilliant discs of light had appeared on the track straight ahead!

And they were getting closer...

...and closer!

   ...and *closer*!!

Chapter 3

Seconds later, the sound of an angry, roaring engine could be heard. Whatever sort of vehicle it was, it was being driven wildly down the sloping track, and was closing fast on them.

"Press the accelerator, Jamie!" his father shouted, leaning over and grasping the steering wheel. "We've got to get out of its way!"

Jamie reached for the pedal and pushed it with his toe. The Land Rover jerked forward and Mr Dawson guided it into the gorse on Jamie's side. With a crunch of snapping branches it plunged into the mass of brilliantly illuminated gold. It was more or less completely off the track, all but for the very back.

Closer and closer the growling vehicle rushed, until the whole track and forest seemed to turn from night into day in its dazzling headlights.

Mr Dawson, in one great heave, pulled Jessica over from her window and deposited her roughly next to her brother.

In a split second, the pair of wild, flaring lights were upon them...and then *crash!!!*...the vehicle clipped the back corner as it whooshed by, and roared away with screeching tyres down the track...and was gone!

The sudden explosion of sound inside the vehicle, as the impact rocked it, terrified all three of its passengers, but in a moment, everything was still and quiet.

"Are you two OK?" asked a rather shaken Mr Dawson, with a tremor in his voice.

Jessica slowly sat up and swept back her long, copper hair.

Still trembling from the experience, she nodded her head and hugged her father.

"I'm alright, but no thanks to those idiots!" she exclaimed angrily.

Mr Dawson leaned over and patted Jamie's ginger mop of hair.

"How about you, son?" he asked.

"That made the dodgems at Whitby Fair look a bit tame!" he said at last, with a grin. "Who *were* those guys?"

"Poachers! Deer poachers!" replied his father. "And mark my words, I'll be in touch with the police as soon as we get home!"

Thoughts of the beautiful roe deer they'd seen in the forest immediately flashed through the children's minds, especially the young albino, the Aqua Crystans called *Chandar* and the young stag they'd met at Christmas, *Strike*.

"Did you catch sight of them?" Jessica asked.

"No, not really, the lights were too bright, but it was a huge blue pick-up truck they were driving, the size of a tank!"

"It felt like a tank, too!" said Jamie. "And have you noticed that our engine's stopped?"

Mr Dawson climbed out and, in the yellow glow of the gorse bushes, inspected the back of the Land Rover.

"She's badly dented and one set of rear lights is totally smashed!" he shouted.

He then managed to open Jamie's door and squeezed into the driver's seat by his son. He turned the ignition. The engine spluttered into life...but then died.

He tried once more, but this time there was no response at all.

"I'm afraid we're going to have to walk back to *Deer Leap*!" he said, thumping his fist angrily on the steering wheel. "The impact must have damaged something in the engine. I'll come back and fix it in the morning."

"But what about all the shopping?" Jessica asked. "We can't just leave it here, can we?"

"Well, let's put it this way, Jess," said her dad, "we're not lumping that lot through the forest! It'll be safe enough. I'm sure that pick-up won't be back tonight. They wouldn't risk it!"

So, with all the doors securely locked, and with one torch from the emergency kit between them, they began the two mile trek home. Mr Dawson knew *George's* tracks like the back of his hand, and with Jamie in charge of the torch, they made good progress across the spruceland. By half-past-nine they were nearly half way to *Deer Leap* and as they came to a junction between two tracks, Jessica suggested they should have a rest on a fallen tree.

It was now absolutely pitch black. Clouds had built up in the sky, and there wasn't a star to be seen. The moon was nowhere in sight.

Jamie turned the torch off to see just how dark it was. They could hardly make out one another as they sat there in the middle of the forest.

There wasn't a sound.

Everything was as still...and as quiet as a graveyard.

"Switch that torch on, Jamie!" snapped Jessica. "It's spoo..!"

It was then that they heard it!

The nightingale.

Silhouetted once again against total silence, the amazing, wonderful tune filled the air. First the same, rapid *'tuk, tuk, weets'* and then the passionate melody of loud shrill notes.

They listened in the darkness, enthralled by the music. Even Jessica's fear vanished as the notes seemed to call her. She felt the same feeling as Jamie had sensed during the hot afternoon. There was a message in the song! Then, her fingers, almost with a will of their own, touched the charms on her necklace. Once again, exactly the same as had happened during the history lesson at school, she felt her fingertips tingle like nettle stings!

The nightingale suddenly stopped as sharply as it had begun, and silence returned to the forest.

"Dad, we've just *got* to see it!" Jessica said at last, breaking the eerie quietness.

Jamie switched on the torch, and its strong beam lit the tall spruce trees that surrounded them almost completely.

"Please, dad, can we try and..?"

"Sshh! There it goes again!" whispered Jamie.

The same tune pierced the warm, forest air, but this time from slightly further away.

Jessica and Jamie were having exactly the same thoughts.

The nightingale was trying to lead them somewhere!

It all made sense!

The tingling charms, the jay feather, the song that seemed to find them wherever they were in the forest. They just *had* to follow the nightingale!!

But, of course, the odds were stacked against them!

Dad wanted to get back to *Deer Leap*, it was pitch black, it seemed as though a storm would break at any moment and Jamie had been ill the night before!

Mr Dawson shook his head.

"Look, kids, we'll come back tomorrow," he said as he stood up. "That's a promise!"

Jessica and Jamie knew there was no point in arguing. So, with Jamie leading the way with the torch, they trudged on homeward.

But they also knew that they were resisting the magic of *Aqua Crysta*! Somehow, they had both felt touched by its power, as though their secret underground realm was calling them. As they walked along the track, they wondered whether if they denied the enticing spell, then the Aqua Crystans would have nothing more to do with them. They would be cut

off, deserted by their friends. They were certain they didn't want that!
If only something would happen to make their father change his mind.
Another sign.

They hadn't long to wait!

Suddenly the three of them stopped, frozen in their tracks!

The beam of the torch had fallen on a sight that made even Mr Dawson
gasp in astonishment.

There, straight ahead of them, nestled on the ground was a young deer,
an albino deer, almost glowing ghostly white in the beam of light.

It seemed to be licking one of its hind legs and was oblivious to the
sudden human intrusion. It raised its head, its pink eyes gleaming ruby
red. Then, it struggled to its feet, and limped off the track and onto a
winding path edged with one of the forest's many ruined walls.

This was the sign Jessica and Jamie had been waiting for!

The deer was unmistakably *Chandar*!

The magic was with them, and, as though to confirm it, they heard, once
again, the song of the nightingale coming from just along the same
narrow path.

"It's the albino youngster we saw last Summer when we'd just moved
here!" whispered Mr Dawson, as Jamie's beam followed it into
the trees.

"Dad, please can we help it?" pleaded Jessica. "*Please?*"

Their father was unable to resist. Memories of Jessica caring for injured
and orphaned young deer back in Scotland with Ruth, and for years after
she died, compelled him to nod his head.

"Alright, alright, I give in!" he whispered.

Jessica and Jamie felt their hearts leap. The magic had worked!

"But listen carefully," their father went on, "I don't want you getting
lost. You haven't got your maps of the forest with you, but if you
follow that path you'll come to a large pond, almost a small lake.
Don't go any further. Understand?"

Both children nodded excitedly, their thoughts already with where the
nightingale, and now *Chandar* would be leading them.

"That wall borders the path all the way so you can't go wrong,"
Mr Dawson continued. "If the storm breaks, there's a ruined barn by the
lake. Make sure you shelter in it. OK?"
Again the children nodded, almost straining at the leash, anxious to be
caught in the magical web that was being woven around them.
"You take the torch. I can manage the rest of the way home without it,"
he added. "This track leads to the country lane only a couple of minutes
from *Deer Leap*. So make sure you come back this way! Got it?"
For the last time, Jessica and Jamie nodded.
"We'll be back as soon as we can," assured Jessica, giving her father a
hug.
"I'll make sure of that," insisted Jamie. "It's m' birthday tomorrow!"
"Yes, and I've got a special surprise waiting for you!" said his dad with
a grin.
"So make sure you're back in good time or I might just change my mind
about it!"

With that, Mr Dawson watched as Jessica and Jamie
took to the path, the torch beam bouncing ahead of them like a great,
white magic wand. He could just make out the albino deer in the
distance as he called a final farewell and started his last lap home.
Meanwhile, Jessica and Jamie delved deeper among
the towering trees, their thick trunks glowing bright green in the light.
Chandar kept some distance ahead, but already the children had noticed
she'd lost her limp. It had all been part of the woven spell.
The nightingale, always out of sight, also played its part by singing its
song now and again, like some kind of magical signpost pointing the
way.
The path wound gently on and on under the
overhanging evergreen branches of the spruce trees. It seemed almost
like two narrow parallel paths in parts with a humped ridge of long grass
between. It wasn't long before Jessica realised it was part of the ancient
horse and cart road they'd discovered near the secret well the Summer

before. As she walked along, following Jamie, she imagined four-in-hand stagecoaches speeding over the moors, long before the trees were planted, their wheels a whirling, spinning blur, the clatter of hooves and the occasional crack of the coachman's whip.

"I wonder if the pond dad was on about was a watering hole for the horses?" she mumbled as she walked on, but Jamie was too busy keeping an eye on *Chandar* to answer.

Another volley of musical notes told them they were still heading in the right direction, and it wasn't long before the path began to slope down into a small valley. Jamie's torch beam lit a smooth, shimmering, silver mirror nestled snugly among the trees. It was the pond, although, as their father had said, it was more like a small lake. Beyond it the path climbed out of the woody dale.

With their eyes attracted to the almost circular, gleaming patch of water, they didn't notice *Chandar* disappear into the dark ranks of spruce trees. She had once again fulfilled her task within the spell. This was where she had lead them.

She and the nightingale.

The lake was the meeting place.

On a branch overhanging the far side of the silver pool, sat the little brown and creamy white bird singing to its heart's content.

Jamie, for the first time managed to train his beam on it, and in the full glare of the spotlight the tiny creature gave another virtuoso performance.

The babbling warble was louder than ever, perhaps enhanced by the reflective water below and by the enclosed nature of the valley.
The melody captivated the children as they listened.
They were entranced by its beauty.
Was this magic or reality?
It was difficult to separate the two, but Jessica and Jamie knew instinctively that, whatever it was, the enchantment had conjured them to the lake...and, although its purpose was far from clear, they knew that something would happen...soon.
The nightingale reached its fluting crescendo...
and then fell silent. The first movement of a natural symphony was over.
The children waited in the darkness for whatever was coming next.

Jamie turned off the torch, making the blackness thicker and heavier than ever.
All was silent.
There wasn't a sound to be heard.
They waited for what seemed an eternity, but actually was just a handful of seconds.
And then, all at once...the conductor raised his baton...and the second movement began!

Chapter 4

It started with the gentle pitter patter, pitter patter, pitter patter of raindrops on the silvery, glossy pool, like a thousand dripping taps. Instantly, the lake's face was transformed from smooth, flawless glass into a myriad of moving, merging ripples...each and every raindrop giving birth to its own ever growing perfect circle of motion which lived and died in a matter of moments as each spread into the next.

Within seconds, there was no room for ripples, as the full curtain of rain was drawn across the lake. The water stirred into a seething ferment of sparkling fizzle like a bubbling, boiling witch's cauldron. Individual pitter patters faded to be replaced by the almost solid roar of a waterfall, a cascade from the sky and as high as the clouds.

The maestro with the baton then signalled the most powerful percussion of all. After his crack of lightning, the tympany of the surging lake was suddenly dwarfed by the mightiest bass drum in the whole of creation! Thunder rolled across the sky, exploding the heavens!

The first strike, though, was a mere rumble compared to the second, which shook the trees to their roots. Then a tremendous crash of clashing cymbals turned night into day, as a huge streak of jagged lightning crackled through the blackness of the night splitting it into two, and heralding the third thunderous explosion which seemed to rock the Earth to its core.

Expecting another fork of lightning to tear across the sky, Jessica and Jamie, both soaking wet, made a dash for the ruined barn which was just off the track. But, as they reached it, to their surprise, the drama ceased as abruptly as it had began.

There was no more lightning, no more thunder and the heavy curtain of pouring rain drew away leaving just the gentle pitter patter on the face of the pool. And then even that slowed and stopped until there remained just the odd drip from overhanging branches splashing into the water.

As the clouds above cleared, stars began to twinkle in the ocean of blackness, and then a full moon emerged from a silver lining and appeared to chase the remaining clouds across the sky. All below was bathed in a silvery sheen as the soft moonlight lit the glistening wet tree trunks, ferns fronds and drifts of pine needles. The air became cooler and heavy with the scents of pine and almond from the clumps of gorse.

Suddenly, the third movement of the symphony began.

A single, solitary note from a distant horn...a sound that meant only one thing to Jessica and Jamie, who peered from the barn straining to hear from where it was coming.

It was the sound of *Aqua Crysta*!

Another adventure was about to begin!

Beneath the sailing moon, ripples began to appear from the edge of the lake just beyond the barn. There seemed to be an inlet into the pool from between the lowest stones of an ancient, moss covered wall.

Another long, single horn note sounded, this time closer.

Jessica and Jamie gasped and quietly pointed as a small boat, no longer than a matchbox, suddenly appeared and glided serenely across the lakes's silver face. Three tiny oars on each side gently lapped the water, as the six oarsmen rhythmically pulled the vessel through the silvery sheen.

Sitting at the prow of the boat was the tiny unmistakable figure of Queen Venetia, with her long, golden hair cascading from her gold coronet. At the stern, hand on the tiller, sat the Deputy Mayor of Pillo, Lepho, his hood folded down and chain of office glinting in the moonbeams. Between them was a third figure, as if asleep, lying on a raised bed of tiny, white flower petals. It was Merrick, the oldest citizen of *Aqua Crysta* and Mayor of Pillo, his dark purple cloak and snowy white hair and beard, again unmistakable.

The boat glided silently across the smooth silver water and seemed to be heading for a small island of reeds near the far side. When it arrived, and had moored by its shore, the oars were withdrawn and the six oarsman calmly lifted the still figure of Merrick on his bed of flowers. Queen Venetia stepped ashore, followed by the short procession of the cloaked oarsmen carrying Merrick's bed on their shoulders, and then Lepho, his ginger head solemnly bowed.

As they vanished from view, hidden by the reeds, another horn note sounded from the inlet, but this time followed by the beginnings of a mournful chorus of scores of voices. The song the voices sang had no words. It was simply tones of sadness and regret, like a slow, medieval, monastic chant.

Tears welled in the eyes of Jessica and Jamie.

They began to understand what they were witnessing...the funeral of their good friend, Merrick...the old, old man who, as a boy, had fled the flames and plague of London in the year 1666.

It was all beginning to make sense.

Merrick had died during the Upper World afternoon.

Whilst the sun had been beating down, Jessica had magically felt his passing during the history lesson about the Great Fire. She had felt the charms tingle at the very moment he had died.

And, at the same instance in time, Jamie had seen and heard the nightingale in the forest. He'd felt the silence and observed the strange presentation of the blue wing feather by the jay. *Aqua Crysta's* mystic powers had reached them, and called and guided them to Merrick's final ceremony...his funeral.

Without saying a word, they listened to the solemn notes as they seemed to fill the little valley, and watched the small boat bobbing gently at its mooring. The boat...of course, they both gradually realised...was the red rowing boat they had brought back with them from the Summer of 1954...the one Dodo had taken from the beach at Sandsend...the one that had carried them and the Magwitches through the sea-cave on the tide and then through the *Cave of Torrents*. It seemed to be a darker colour now, but it was definitely the same little boat.

The chanting began to fade as the island mourners returned to the shore and climbed aboard their funeral vessel. The last notes disappeared as the oarsmen dipped their oars into the lake and ferried the Queen and Lepho back towards the inlet at the foot of the wall.

The funeral was over.

The children wondered what was going to happen next.

Did the Aqua Crystans even realise they were in the tumbledown barn watching them?

They didn't have to wait long to find out.

As the little boat neared the inlet, Lepho guided it to a flat, mossy stone that had fallen from the wall and was now gently lapped by the pond's water.

A couple of the oarsmen jumped ashore in the moonlight and held the craft steady as the Queen and Lepho stepped onto the stone.

They seemed to be looking around the edge of the lake as though they were expecting visitors.

Jessica walked slowly from the barn as calmly as possible so as not to alarm the tiny, thumb-sized figures. Jamie carefully followed, feeling like a giant in such small company. They both knelt by the wall and peered down at their magical hosts.

They looked so small and fragile. Drooping above them were half a dozen very early bluebell flowers looking like a posy of leaning ornate, old fashioned lamp-posts, each with its smooth green stem and bell decorated with glistening rain drops. The Queen and Lepho were hardly bigger than the delicate bunches of bells and were dwarfed even more by a large spreading fern frond that swept upwards behind the flowers. Lepho noticed their guests first, smiled and gestured a welcome with his arm.

The Queen, in her long green gown, then walked over to him and gazed up at the huge, familiar faces looking over the remaining stones of the wall.

She spoke, and although her voice seemed distant, the children could hear every word she said.

"Greetings once more, to our friends from the Upper World!" she began, with her usual grace. "You will have seen that the occasion is a sad one for us all, but it was the honourable Merrick's wish that you attend his last journey to his beloved island...the one he called Avalon. It was also his wish that you be summoned to hopefully fulfill his last request, one that is of great significance to the whole realm of *Aqua Crysta*, and one that, we alone, would find beyond our powers to accomplish."

She paused and signalled for a small chest to be brought to her from the boat.

As she opened it to reveal its contents, Lepho knelt before her, and she continued.

"Your friend and fellow adventurer, Lepho, will relate more of this matter to you in time, but first I have a royal duty to perform on behalf of all the people of *Aqua Crysta!*"

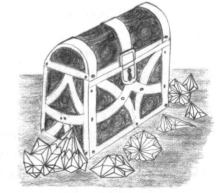

She carefully lifted from the chest the golden chain and medallion which Merrick had proudly worn for more than one and a half Upper World centuries - the insignia of the Mayor of Pillo, the second most important office in *Aqua Crysta*, after the position of the Queen herself.

Lepho bowed his head and swept back his hood.

The Queen carefully placed the chain over his shoulders, and as he stood, another single note from a hidden horn in the passageway broke the silence to be followed by a much more exalting chorus from the concealed choir.

The solemn chant that had accompanied Merrick's funeral had been replaced by one of melodic, joyous praise and celebration.

The Queen then embraced her new second-in-command, and made a graceful beckoning gesture towards the mouth of the inlet. Two familiar figures stepped onto the mossy stone, which brought instant smiles to the faces of the watching Jessica and Jamie. It was wonderful for them to see once again their best friends, Jonathan and Jane, the brother and sister from the 1950's, who had lived in *Aqua Crysta* for fifty harvests but had hardly aged a single year.

Jane, with her pigtails and summer frock and sandals shook Lepho's hand in congratulation and then waved wildly at the two enormous beaming faces beyond the tumbledown wall.

Jonathan, in his sleeveless pullover, khaki shorts and sandals did the same. Jessica and Jamie waved back, as the melodic singing faded and the Queen spoke once more.

"Re-united once more, our realm's heroic adventurers!" she proclaimed. "Ready to fulfill Merrick's dying wish, so that he may rest in peace for ever."

Jessica and Jamie, still completely puzzled by the Queen's words, but magically enticed into carrying out whatever she asked, strained forward to listen. Her words gave no inkling, no hint, of what lay ahead - Lepho was charged with that - but, for now, it was clear that Jessica and Jamie must first take Lepho, Jonathan and Jane with them, away from the lake and to a place of safety in the Upper World. There, the whole nature of Merrick's last request would be explained.

Queen Venetia wished her heroes well, taking in turn the hands of Lepho, Jonathan and Jane and blowing a kiss to the giant Jessica and Jamie. Then she turned and walked towards the inlet. With one last backward glance and a smile, she disappeared from view.

The five were left alone by the lakeside, the moon still racing across the blackness of the night.
Even the nightingale had vanished.
All was quiet.

As arranged, Lepho, Jonathan and Jane pulled the boat up onto the stone and climbed aboard. Jamie then slowly reached over the mossy rocks of the wall and picked it up. Carefully he placed it on the palm of his left hand and he and his sister looked at its tiny passengers.

"Have you considered a place of safety until our journey begins?" asked Lepho. "There I can tell you more of Merrick's last request."
"We certainly have!" replied Jessica. "But it'll mean a half-hour trek through the forest. It might be a bit of a bumpy ride!"
"Bumpy my foot!" protested Jamie. "You'll be travelling first-class!" he assured the three Aqua Crystans.
"Anything will be smoother than those voyages through the sea-cave and the *Cave of Torrents*!" laughed Jonathan, remembering the last time he travelled in the boat.

Jessica, with the torch, lead the way back along the path leaving the enchanting lake behind. It was quite slippery underfoot after the storm, but Jamie managed to keep the tiny boat steady on his left hand with the other cupped over it. Just once he nearly lost his balance when he tripped over a tree root, but the passengers grabbed the sides of the boat tightly and no-one fell overboard!
Soon they reached the track where they had left Mr Dawson, and the going became easier and quicker as Jessica and Jamie headed for home. The sky by now was a mass of twinkling stars. All the clouds had gone and the moon seemed to be still, hovering above the tops of the trees

like a bright, white balloon.

"It's so clear tonight," said Jamie, as he stared up into the blackness, with his hands cupped in front of him as though he was holding a pet mouse.

"You just watch where you're walking!" called back his sister from a few paces in front, although she too had noticed the stars. The majestic, sweeping *Plough* constellation was directly above them...pointing, as always, to the *North Star*. Jessica gazed past it towards the great letter '*W*' of *Queen Cassiopeia* but, now, at this time of the year, her daughter *Princess Andromeda* and the enormous square of *Pegasus* were out of sight.

Jessica dreamily recalled how she'd seen the great pictures in the night sky the Summer before...the albino deer jumping over a wall, the candle flame called *Lumina* and the giant, white-bearded face...all as clear as crystal and all framed within the four corners of *Pegasus*. That was when the secret magical adventures had begun...what seemed like ages ago...

Suddenly, with no warning, a huge beam of light swept across the treetops blotting out the moon and the stars.

Instantly, Jessica and Jamie stopped and turned.

There, some way back down the track, they could see a single enormous, powerful spotlamp. It was just hanging in the air, but its beam was sweeping from side to side, lighting up the ranks of trees on each side of the track.

As Jessica and Jamie stood, motionless, transfixed by the beam, it suddenly fell upon *them*...the brilliance dazzling their eyes.

Then the frightening roar of an engine bursting into life shattered the silence!

Two more brilliant lights flashed on, beneath the single one!

"It's the deer poachers!" yelled Jessica. *"They've seen us!"*

The trio of beams bouncing wildly towards them,

together with the roar of the ferocious engine, stung them out of their trance.

"*Quick*! *Hide*!" shouted Jamie, as they both dived for cover beside the track.

But the downpour had made the dust on the surface of the track greasy and slippery.

Closer and closer the three-eyed monster bore down on them!

Suddenly, as he was just about to spring off the track, Jamie's trainers lost their grip and he plunged headlong into the rough verge.

His hand's precious cargo was catapulted into the air.

Jamie glanced back at the track, now its glistening surface shining yellowy gold in the lightbeams.

To his horror he could see the tiny boat, upside down, a couple of paces away on the track, right in the path of the pick-up truck!

He was helpless to do anything!

They were both helpless to do anything!

Jessica, realising what had happened, covered her face. She couldn't bear to look.

The great, angry spinning tyres would be on the boat at any moment!

It was too late to do anything!

The boat would be smashed to smithereens!

Then with a wild flurry of light, noise, dust and wind, the monster roared past, and was gone into the night.

As its evil, grinding, skidding din faded in the distance, together with its red rear-lights, Jessica squinted through the bars of her fingers over her face and shone the torchbeam into the clouds of settling dust just above the track.

She hoped and prayed with all her heart that the very worst hadn't happened.

Slowly, and in eerie silence, the swirling yellow began to clear...

Chapter 5

"Don't move!" Jessica whispered as her brother began to stir from his fall.

"They could be anywhere, and they're so small!"

Keeping herself as still as she could, she trained the torchbeam on the track.

Standing out clearly were the freshly laid prints of the pick-up's tyre treads, their harsh, sharp zigzags almost sizzling and spitting like a pair of angry vipers.

There was no sign of the boat.

Jessica slowly stood up without moving her feet, and shone the beam on the tyre tracks from a greater height.

She suddenly gasped at what she saw!

For there, nestled in the middle of the nearer of the two tracks, were the splintered, flattened remains of the tiny rowing boat, the broken bits of brown, black and red wood beyond any recognition. Jessica and Jamies' hearts sank at the thought of what had happened to the three Aqua Crystans who had trusted them to find a place of safety.

They were speechless as the full horror swept over them, like some kind of cold, thick mist. They both felt saddened and sickened to the core.

A feeling of such deep sorrow they had never felt before in their lives.

They realised that they were to blame for the deaths of their three closest friends.

The weight of guilt was so heavy it felt as though their feet were being pushed into the forest floor.

Jessica, desperate to catch sight of their friends and hoping they had been thrown from the boat, cast the torchbeam among the stalks of long, coarse grass and clumps of yellow coltsfoot. But there was no sign of any of them.

She knew, in her heart of hearts, that the task was likely to be a fruitless one, but growing panic and guilt kept her searching while Jamie kept as still as he could.

The beam explored frantically between every blade of grass, around every small rock.

But still it found no-one.

"Just a sec! What was that?" called Jamie. "Shine it back a few inches!"

Jessica guided the beam back by a clump of budding ragweed, and they both noticed a glistening, winding silver thread on the ground.

"It's just a snail trail," sighed Jessica.

She traced it to a drooping coltsfoot and then carefully bent down and used her hand to move its jagged, heart-shaped leaves to one side.

There, nestled beneath, was the snail with its brown and cream spiral patterned shell.

"We're here!"came a tiny voice.

Jessica's heart leapt as the three tiny figures emerged from behind the shell, each one groggily waving and shielding dazzled eyes from the bright torchbeam.

With the great weight of guilt removed, Jessica slid her hand through the leaves and let Lepho, Jonathan and Jane, one by one, climb onto her palm.

She stood up slowly and then looked at the shaken Aqua Crystans as they sat among the lines of her hand. Jamie, rather sheepishly got to his feet and looked at his three tiny friends.

"I'm so very, very sorry about that!" he whispered, although he knew no words could possibly convey his relief.

"It wasn't your fault, Master Jamie!" uttered Lepho, as he brushed yellow dust from his purple cloak. "But we are, all three, glad to be alive! Where is the boat? Let us continue with our journey!"

"The boat was crushed flat by the deer poachers' truck," explained Jessica as gently as she could. "But we'll soon be at *Deer Leap*, our cottage. You'll be able to recover there!"

So, with the Aqua Crystans safely snuggled in Jessica's cupped hands and Jamie in charge of the torch, they made their way along the track which lead to the lane near *Deer Leap*. Thankfully, there were no further mishaps, and they all hoped that they wouldn't encounter the monstrous truck again!

They didn't, and much to their relief they were soon walking along *Deer Leap's* grassy track, the full moon still sailing across the black night sky.

"Dad's left the lights on for us," whispered Jamie as he and his sister approached the cottage.

"I hope he's left the front door unlocked as well!" said Jessica as they reached the porch.

He had, so quietly Jessica pushed open the door, making sure it didn't squeak and together the two children tiptoed down the hallway between the front room and their dad's study.

Suddenly, and scaring the life out of Jessica and Jamie, the study door opened and out stepped their father in his blue dressing gown and slippers.

"The wanderers return at last!" he beamed. "I was expecting you back an hour ago. I bet you got soaked in that storm!"

"We did, but we sheltered from the worst of it in the barn you told us about," said Jessica. "But we lost the deer!"

"I hope you didn't come across those maniacs again!"

"N...no, we didn't!" stuttered Jamie, trying to hide the truth. "Hope we haven't kept you up. We thought you'd be in bed!"

"No, I had a spot of paperwork to catch up on so I thought I'd wait up for you."

Mr Dawson suddenly noticed Jessica's cupped hands.

"What've you got there?" he asked curiously, rubbing his bearded chin.

"It's just a..."

"A snail!" burst Jamie, realising their precious secret was in danger.

"Not another Brian!" laughed his dad, remembering the pet snail Jessica had kept in Scotland.

"No this one's Sidney!" said Jessica, peeping through a gap in her hands above her thumb. "You can meet him tomorrow!"

"Talking of tomorrow, it's almost Jamie's *Big Day!*" said Mr Dawson, glancing at the clock on the mantelpiece in the front room.

"I suggest you two get that damp clothing off and get a good night's sleep! Do you want any supper, or a hot drink or something?"

"No thanks, dad!" chorused Jessica and Jamie as they nearly tripped over one another on the stairs.

"Goodnight, then!" said Mr Dawson, amazed at his children's sudden urgent desire to get to bed. "See you in the morning!"

Jessica's bedside set of drawers proved to be an ideal hotel for her tiny guests. The top floor was full of all sorts of things that she had collected and hoarded away over the years - rings, bracelets and necklaces, not to mention old coins, photos of her mother, postcards, foreign stamps, a sewing kit, a set of watercolour paints, pencils and odd felt-tips. It was a real hotchpotch, but there was one  object that Jonathan and Jane immediately noticed as soon as they had jumped off Jessica's hand...and that was a large chunk of greenish white crystal wedged between a couple of curly ammonite fossils and some periwinkle shells.

"That's from the Gargoyle's time-tunnel, isn't it?" exclaimed Jonathan, pointing up at the glassy crystal which towered above him.

Jessica knelt down on her rug and gazed into the drawer, entranced by the sight of her three tiny friends exploring her memories. "I kept it as a souvenir from our last great adventure!" she whispered.

Lepho, leaning against a huge pink ribbon hairslide, looked up at Jessica's enormous face.

"I see you've got quite a collection of jay feathers too!" he beamed, pointing at about a dozen blue quills in a pile.

"They're from the garland that was around Strike's neck when we met him on Christmas night at the Dell," Jessica explained, as she unfastened her charm necklace and laid it carefully on a small square of purple velvet.

"I hope it all makes you feel at home!"

Jane rushed over and touched the tiny charms one by one.

"I'm sure I recognise the chain as well!" she said, holding the silver goblet.

"It's one of the chains that held those monster digging machines as they were lowered from the sky next to *Old Soulsyke*! Do you remember?"

Jane nodded as she thought of the fun they'd had shrinking the huge machines with the magic froth from the buckets of pump water. She burst out laughing when she remembered the soldiers' faces when they were being haunted by the trees!

"I bet you don't know what these are!" laughed Jamie as he carefully fingered five tiny, beautiful shimmering droplets of glassy violet and turquoise tucked behind the periwinkles.

Jonathan picked one up in his arms and shook his head as did the others. Each small crystal tube was almost transparent with lots of glistening faces and edges.

"Give us a clue!" grinned Jonathan, looking puzzled.

"Something we saw in the passage beyond the *Cave of Torrents* before we came to the *Star Cavern*!" suggested Jessica with a twinkle in her eye. Still, the three visitors shook their heads, curiously inspecting the strange objects.

"Something that buzzed and flew round our heads!" laughed Jamie.
"What, something to do with the *crystalids*!" gasped Jane at last, remembering the fantastic flying creatures they encountered on their last adventure.
"We reckon they're *crystalid eggs*...!" beamed Jamie. "We hope they hatch one day! We found them in Jessie's bobcap when we got back here on Christmas Day!"
"According to legend," pointed out Lepho, looking inquisitively for any sign of life in one of the crystals, "they take two or three harvests to hatch...but, you never know, things might just happen with greater speed here in the Upper World. You shall have to wait and see!"

At that moment, Jessica heard the familiar eerie creak of the third step from the top of the stairs.
"What's that?" exclaimed Jonathan, hiding behind one of the ammonite fossils.
"It's just...," began Jessica, as a gentle tap was heard on her bedroom door.
She sprang up from the rug, turned and quickly shoved the drawer closed, sending her guests tumbling among the hotchpotch!
The door opened and in stepped her father in his dressing gown clutching a large, old margarine tub.
"I've put some rocks and soil in here for Sidney!" he announced enthusiastically. "Best make him feel at home!"
"Oh, thanks, dad. It's just the job!" said Jessica, rushing over to take it from her father.
"Where is he then?" he asked, looking round the bedroom.
"I've...I've just put him in..."
Suddenly, there was a long, groaning moan from the landing and Jamie appeared with an anguished expression on his face and his hands clenching his stomach.
"Oh, dad, I feel bad again!" he gasped.
Mr Dawson put an arm around his son's shoulders and lead him to the

41

door mumbling something about fish and chips and a hot water bottle for his upset stomach. Just as he was about to disappear, Jamie glanced back at Jessica and smiled and winked. His rescue act had worked! Their secret was safe!

When the coast was clear, Jessica peeped into her top drawer and was relieved to see Lepho, Jonathan and Jane sitting on a green rubber near the large crystal. Lepho's tiny voice suddenly rang out, made louder by a cavernous whelk shell just behind him.

"Can I relate to you the details of our quest?" he asked.

"If we just wait a few minutes, dad'll be in bed, and then I'll tap on the wall for Jamie."

"But I thought he was unwell?" asked Lepho.

"No, he's perfectly OK!" laughed Jessica. "He could win an Oscar for his acting!"

"Who is this...Oscar?" wondered a rather puzzled Lepho.

"Oh, that's another story!" laughed Jessica again. "Just wait until the grandfather clock downstairs strikes midnight. Then you can tell us both your tale. I can hardly wait!"

As the chimes on the hour broke the night's silence in *Deer Leap*, Jessica gently tapped on her bedroom wall. The signal for Jamie to creep into her room. A few seconds later, her door slowly opened and in tiptoed Jamie. He quietly closed the door and Jessica switched on her bedside lamp. In the pinky white light they both knelt on the rug in their pyjamas and Jessica carefully slid the top drawer open. They moved closer and closer and gazed into the jumble...but there was no sign at all of Lepho, Jonathan nor Jane!

"Jane!" whispered Jessica. "Where are you? Jonathan! Are you there?" As they looked into every likely nook and cranny, thoughts flashed through their minds about the Aqua Crystans perhaps having fled because they felt unsafe.

"They must be here *somewhere*!" whispered Jamie. "They can't have vanished into thin air!"

"I wouldn't put it past them with all their magical powers!" sighed Jessica, looking among her coils of beads.

But just then, Jamie caught sight of movement near the rubber.

"There they are!" he pointed as the tiny trio emerged one by one from the spiralled whelk shell.

"Our apologies, Jessica and Jamie!" said Lepho. "But we couldn't resist exploring! It's wonderful in there!"

"It was like being in the sea-cave at Sandsend!" Jane enthused. "The roar of the sea was terrific!"

"We thought for a minute you'd magically disappeared!" Jessica admitted.

"No, we're still here!" laughed Lepho. "And I'm eager to relate my story, so let me begin!"

The three Aqua Crystans made themselves comfortable by the charm necklace on the plush carpet of velvet and then Lepho began.

His tale was amazing, astonishing...the best bedtime story Jessica, Jamie, Jonathan and Jane had ever heard!

But was it true?

Was it possible that Merrick's twin sisters had not died all those centuries ago when they had lived as orphans with the cruel Master of Soulsyke? That instead they had run away and found shelter in caves to the south?

Caves that had yielded life preserving golden waters which sustained them for hundreds of years?

"But it sounds as though they found another *Aqua Crysta*!" gasped Jessica. "Another place founded on magical underground water!"

"But are they still alive?" burst Jamie, as loudly as he dared. "What are their names?"

Lepho raised his arms in an attempt to stop the questions.

"There is much more to tell!" he smiled. "If you are patient, your questions will be answered, but there is much that Merrick left unanswered and it is to those questions we have to address our mission!"

He took a deep breath and continued.

"Hester and Gwenda, Merrick's sisters, lived in the caves, almost as hermits, for years upon years and made a living by welcoming strangers from all parts of Upper World England who wanted to bathe in their golden waters. Eventually, crowds of people visited the caves, day after day, year after year, as medical men proclaimed the water's value for easing and curing many ailments. It all became too much for the sisters, especially when they began to be regarded as freakish oddities because they appeared so young despite being well over a hundred years old. So it came to pass that in the year 1778 they vanished and were never seen again. The bathing stopped and the tracks to the caves became overgrown and forgotten!"

Lepho paused and took another deep breath.

"Now comes the most important part of my tale, and the part that has urged Queen Venetia to act on behalf of all the inhabitants of *Aqua Crysta!*"

He paused again, stood and paced around in a circle looking anxious. He stopped and leaned against a silver pencil sharpener on the edge of the velvet carpet.

He began again.

"Just after the last frosts of Winter had melted, a few weeks ago in your Upper World time, Merrick received a message. A message from his sisters whom he thought had died as children over three centuries ago! The words were written in golden ink on ancient parchment and had been delivered, according to the message, in the talons of '*a mighty bird from Needle Crag*'. The rolled parchment had been found, incidentally, by the first food foraging party of the Spring at the entrance to the Harvest Passageway, near the hidden well-head."

"What else did the message say?" gasped Jamie, almost bursting to find out what the quest was all about.

Lepho once again held up his hands, and paced back and forth on the velvet carpet.

All eyes were fixed on him as he began once again.

"The words on the parchment told Merrick of his own death within weeks and the death of his sisters within hours of their brother's passing away!"

Lepho paused again, and walked over to the gaping mouth of the whelk shell.

His next words almost exploded from the drawer.

"And the message concluded by proclaiming that when all three were dead, the *"lights from the skies that gave never-ending life would return and take back their powerful gift!"*

Lepho sat down, almost exhausted, and put his head in his hands.

His audience was speechless, as his words tossed about in their minds. What could they do?

Could the deaths of the three evacuees from the Great Fire of London end the magical realms of *Aqua Crysta* and the *Golden Waters of Needle Crag*...wherever that was?

And what were the *'lights from the skies'*?

The words mystified them all, and what they could do about them puzzled them even more...but a sudden torrent of musical notes from beyond Jessica's bedroom window, told them that the answer could be near.

It was the nightingale!

They all heard it at once!

Jessica sprang to her feet and dashed as quietly as she could across to the window!

She threw back the curtains...and there...

...before her... on the sill...

...was a sight that made her reel back in horror and cover her eyes!!

This...was no nightingale!!!

Chapter 6

It seemed to fill the whole window, and although it was lit by the glow of the bedroom lamp, it seemed to have a shimmering golden radiance all of its own.

It was a bird, but not one that Jessica or Jamie ever thought they'd see.

Before them, wings spread like enormous, creamy, feathered fans, the width of the window, was a magnificent Eagle Owl. This had to be the '*mighty bird from Needle Crag*', the messenger from the place called the *Golden Waters*!!

Jamie crept over from the bedside as though magnetically drawn by the staring bright, orangy gold eyes which were set like fiery topazes each in its own soft, feathery saucer.

Above them, giving the owl's face an expression of anger and menace, was a furrowed 'V' of darker feathers crowned with a pair of long ear-like tufts.

It was, at one and the same time, both magnificent and threateningly evil.

"What are we going to do?" whispered Jamie, as he inched closer to the window.

The owl watched him intently, as though, but for the window panes, it would strike at any moment.

A sudden beating of its wings against the glass stopped Jamie, but he could now just about see the owl's ferocious talons gripping the edge of the stone window-sill.

"There's something tied to one of its legs!" he gasped.

Jessica stepped forward.

"It's a rolled parchment tied with ribbon!" she burst. "It's another message! We've somehow got to get it! The nightingale must have lead the owl here!"

Slowly, Jessica swept back the left hand curtain, watched all the time by the inquisitive, golden eyes. Then, very, very slowly, she reached for the bottom window bar and lifted it free. With her other hand she pulled the window catch handle downwards, and, after taking a deep breath, gently pushed the side window slightly open. She felt the cool, night air on the back of her hand as the gap widened. All the time, the owl stayed perfectly still, just shuffling along the sill a little to allow the window to open.

Jessica then, with her heart pounding, inched her fingers along the sill towards the vicious, razor sharp talons. Half expecting a sudden flurry of wings and a stabbing thrust from the owl's hooked beak, she pulled at one of the dangling ends of ribbon. Instantly, to her relief, the parchment loosened, and, still very slowly, she grasped the roll and drew it towards her.

It was then that she noticed a small basket, like a miniature wicker laundry basket with a lid, tied to the owl's other leg. But still, she concentrated on sliding the rolled parchment along the sill until she could pull it through the gap of the open window.

With a gasp of excitement and relief, she stepped back from the window and rushed over to her bed with Jamie close behind.

They sat on the edge of the duvet and Jessica carefully unfurled the roll of parchment. As it crinkled and crackled open, Lepho, Jonathan and Jane stood on the rubber in an attempt to see what was going on.

"Read it out so we can hear!" called Jane in a squeaky voice from the top drawer.

"I will, I will!" whispered Jessica. "Just hang on a sec!"

When the parchment was fully unrolled, she put it towards her lamp. The golden handwriting gleamed in the light.

"It's a bit wobbly and spidery," she said, "but here goes!"

"It's for you, Lepho!" she whispered excitedly, glancing down at the tiny trio. "It says at the top...'*To the Mayor of Pillo*'!"

"Come on, Jess! Read it out!" pleaded Jamie, impatiently.

"Hold your horses, Jamie, it's not easy!"

Slowly, Jessica began to read the message.

> *"To the Mayor of Pillo,*
> *Make haste for time is of*
> *the essence!*
> *Fly with Merlyn to Needle Crag.*
> *(You will find carriage*
> *beneath his wings)*
> *Come at once!*
> *The end of your world is nigh!*
> *May your journey be safe!*
> *Hester and Gwenda"*

48

"It's from Merrick's sisters!" exclaimed Lepho. "There's no time to lose! Quickly take me to the carriage!"

"But Lepho, you can't fly off into the night!" said Jessica. "It could be some kind of trick! You could be lost forever, or worse!"

"I have to go!" insisted Lepho. "Please show me the carriage!"

Jessica reluctantly placed her hand into the drawer by the rubber and let the tiny Lepho scramble up onto her little finger and then into her cupped palm.

"You're absolutely sure about this?" she whispered, her giant face dwarfing the miniature figure.

"Yes, yes!" insisted Lepho. "I have to go for Queen Venetia and the people of *Aqua Crysta*! But before I go, can I ask that you find the place called *Needle Crag*, and get there yourselves with Jonathan and Jane. I will need your help, and I am sure the magic that's in the air will help you find me. Will you do that for me and for *Aqua Crysta*?"

"It's a promise!" beamed Jamie. "Of course we will!"

With that, Lepho waved goodbye to his fellow Aqua Crystans in the drawer, and Jessica gently placed him by the open window.

The breeze ruffled his ginger hair and purple cloak as he ran along the stony sill, the great owl towering menacingly above him. He looked so small and helpless as though Merlyn could have him in his beak in a trice like a mere insect morsel of the night.

But, although the owl still looked fearsome, he was obviously safe, tame, trustworthy and even gentle and friendly. Appearances, thought Jessica, can definitely be deceptive!

Suddenly, however, she realised that Lepho was undertaking his journey without a talisman for good fortune. She quickly scampered across the room and picked the smallest jay feather she could find from the pile in the top drawer.

"Wish him luck from us!" called Jonathan, as Jessica darted back to the window and tapped on the bottom pane, just next to Merlyn's talons.

Lepho, who was just about to climb into the basket, spotted the feather and ran back to the open window to take it from Jessica's thumb and forefinger.

"Jonathan and Jane send their good wishes!" Jessica whispered, as Lepho made for his wicker carriage with the feather waving aloft like a banner.

"Good luck to you four as well!" he shouted back. "I'll see you at *Needle Crag!*"

He crawled into the basket, tucked the feather around himself and then gave a final wave before he closed the hinged lid.

With a flurry of those huge wings, Merlyn launched into the night air with his precious cargo strapped beneath. The great wings flapped majestically with fingerlike feathers spread to ensure silence...and a moment later, the golden giant had gone.

Jessica and Jamie gazed above the trees and could just make out the bird's graceful silhouette as he flew amid the stars. They hoped and prayed that Lepho would be safe, and thankfully, something at the back of their minds told them that he would be.

Jessica closed the window and then drew the curtains, thinking constantly how on earth they were going to work out where *Needle Crag* was!

"Any ideas?" she asked her brother, but it was Jane who came up with the first clue.

"When we used to live at *Old Soulsyke* just after the Second World War, there was talk of opening some kind of health-spa a few miles to the south..."

"Oh yes, I remember!" chipped in Jonathan. "Something to do with water with amazing properties which flowed into Newtondale Gorge..."

"But nothing ever came of it!" said Jane. "The whole area was too rough and overgrown."

"You never know," said Jamie. "It sounds like a possibility. I'll nip back to m' room and get a map."

As quietly as he could, he slipped through the door, and seconds later he was back, clutching a large, folded map. He spread it out on the floor, and Jessica switched on her main ceiling light so they could study the fine detail.

"Can we have a look too?" came a voice from nowhere.

"Certainly!" replied Jessica, lowering her hand into the top drawer, and allowing Jonathan and Jane to climb aboard.

Soon the two Aqua Crystans were running along a deep crease in the map, as Jamie's finger pointed to the Newtondale Gorge.

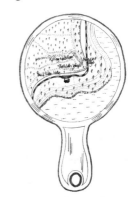

Jessica found her magnifying glass from the top drawer and looked at the close contours of the Gorge, and the words printed around it such as *Killing Nab Scar, Yaul Sike Hole* and *Beulah Wood*. Jonathan and Jane stepped from one place-name to the other. Jessica laughed when she saw them magnified, but Jonathan and Jane got quite a shock when they looked upwards to see Jessica's enormous blue eye peering down at them!

Suddenly, Jamie exclaimed with excitement, "Look, there...*Needle Point* and *Needle Eye*!!"

"Sssh! Dad'll hear!" whispered Jessica, nudging her brother...but it was too late!

The bedroom door burst open and their father walked in with angry, furrowed eyebrows to match Merlyn's!

"What time do you call this?" he shouted. "Do you realise that it's nearly *one o'clock in the morning?*"

But then, to make things a hundred times worse, he caught sight of something...

...something moving!

...something scampering across the spread out map on the floor!!!

Chapter 7

At the very same time as Jonathan and Jane scurried south over whirls of contours and patches of green to evade the astonished eyes of their friend of long-ago Sandsend Summers, Lepho, too, was heading in the same direction.

All was darkness in the basket beneath Merlyn's slowly flapping wings, although, now and again, Lepho caught glimpses through gaps in the wicker of silvery treetops and winding streams way, way below. Never had he ventured so far! Even food foraging expeditions had taken him no further than the copse of woodland around *Old Soulsyke*! But now, he was travelling further than any other of his fellow countrymen had ever travelled in the history of *Aqua Crysta*! No one had ever been higher either, and the more he considered his venture, the more fear of the unknown began to grip him with its icy fingers. All he could do was combat such thoughts, with a determination to carry out dutifully the request of his Queen and the last wishes of Merrick. He had, without fail, to reach Hester and Gwenda and discover the meaning of the '*lights from the skies*' and what it told of the future of his beloved realm.

Jonathan and Jane, meanwhile, had scampered into their own darkness and fear which lay beneath Jessica's bed!

As they crouched behind one of her fluffy slippers, they watched and listened, hearts beating wildly, as Mr Dawson, unable to believe his eyes, knelt down in his pyjamas and lifted the corner of the map.

"I'm sure I saw something move!" he exclaimed.

"It was probably a spider or something!" said Jamie, as coolly and calmly as he could.

"No, it definitely wasn't a spider. It was chunkier, colourful...with four legs and arms...like tiny people!!"

"Dad, I think you've been working too hard!" said Jessica, trying to muster a smile.

"And, what's this?" asked their father, suddenly noticing the curled parchment on the bed.

"It...it's...a hidden treasure game we've invented!" stammered Jamie nervously. "Jess writes the clues on ancient looking paper with her gold ink!"

Luckily, their father was too intent on looking around the floor to bother reading it, but as his hands started feeling around the rug and the foot of the bedside drawers, Jessica and Jamies' hearts were in their mouths! And so were Jonathan and Janes'!

As the huge hands delved towards them under the bed, they quickly darted into the deeper darkness near the skirting board. They were just in time as the gigantic five-legged creature grasped the slipper and dragged it out onto the rug.

"Perhaps whatever it was is in here!" said the increasingly puzzled Mr Dawson as he shook it. Then he grabbed the other and shook that! With nothing appearing, he scratched and shook his head in complete bewilderment, stood up and looked at his children one after the other. "I'm sure I saw something move!" he repeated. "I'm sure I did!"

Jessica and Jamie almost began to feel sorry for him as he quietly turned, and walked towards the door, still shaking his head slowly and muttering to himself.

Before he retreated back to his own bedroom, he turned and glanced at the map on the floor.

"I'm sure I did!" he mumbled. "Oh and by the way, happy birthday, son! I do believe it's Saturday! How's your stomach feeling?"

"Oh, It's OK now, dad!" said Jamie. "The hot-water bottle must have done the trick!"

"I'm glad to hear it," Mr Dawson said, still in a quiet, sort of confused tone.

"Now off you go to bed so you'll be wide awake tomorrow morn... I mean, this morning! Remember, there's a special surprise waiting for you!"

The door closed, and Jessica and Jamie looked at one another, not knowing whether to burst out laughing or feel sympathy for their bewildered father.

"More and more strange things are happening to the poor guy!" whispered Jamie. "He must be getting suspicious by now that there's something funny going on!"

"Well, that little episode was too close for comfort for me!" admitted Jessica. "I suggest we act as normally as possible from now on, or dad's going to start thinking that either he's going round the bend, or his kids are!!"

"Then let's put Jonathan and Jane back in the drawer," suggested Jamie, "and then I'll go to bed and see you tomorrow...I mean today!... and then we can work out how we're going to get to *Needle Crag* and Lepho!"

With that, they both knelt on the rug and Jessica whispered into the darkness under her bed, "Jonathan...Jane...it's safe now! You can come out!"

There was no reply.

"Jonathan! Jane!" she repeated with a note of worry in her voice. There was still no reply.

"Whatever's happened to them?" gasped Jessica, thinking that yet another disaster had befallen the Aqua Crystans.

As they both stared into the darkness, Jamie, at last, saw two tiny figures appearing out of the gloom.

"There they are!" he whispered, but then he nudged his sister and pointed.

It was Jonathan and Jane alright...but they weren't alone!!

Meanwhile, way to the south, beyond the furthest bounds of the pine forest, Merlyn was flying above open moorland and nearing the end of his journey.

Lepho, still wrapped in the comforting jay feather, peeped through a crack in the wicker basket. Ahead, he could just make out the jagged outline of towering, inhospitable looking rocks set against the starry sky. They seemed to soar from a dense forest of grasping, tangled branches of ancient trees not yet fully in leaf.

One particular rock soared higher than the rest, tapering to a point, looking like a giant wolf's fang tooth.

'That must be the *Needle Crag*!' thought Lepho, as Merlyn began to glide closer and closer to the ever-growing, eerie precipice.

At the same time, Jonathan and Jane drew closer and closer to the enormous faces which loomed before them beyond the bed. Both faces beamed as Jessica and Jamie realised what was following the two inch high figures.

"I haven't seen that for ages!" whispered Jamie. "It shows how often *you* clean under your bed!"

"I can't work out what it's doing here in the first place!" Jessica whispered back, giving her brother a sharp nudge with her elbow.

"We found it by the skirting board! It must have slipped down the side of your bed!" called Jonathan. "It's fantastic, isn't it?"

Rolling over the carpet and into the light came the wonderful sight of a vintage van towed on a piece of cotton thread by the two delighted Aqua Crystans.

It was Jamie's scale model of a *Ford 'T'* delivery van, with its black roof, mudguards and running-boards and maroon bodywork. Glinting in the light were its silver radiator, headlamps and bumper bar.

Jonathan and Jane towed it to the edge of the rug, dropped the thread

and excitedly jumped onto the running-boards. A moment later, they had opened the two side doors and perched themselves on the long front seat, with Jane gripping the tiny steering wheel.

"It's wonderful!" called Jane, "and the back doors open as well, so we can sleep in it tonight before we set off tomorrow! Can you put us in the top drawer?"

Jessica carefully lifted the model and both she and Jamie looked into the tiny van with its two passengers. It looked amazing with real people waving wildly at them through the side windows. Then she slowly placed it next to the patch of velvet in her drawer. Jonathan and Jane jumped out, darted round the back and opened the doors.

Jessica quickly pulled a pink tissue from the box next to her bedside lamp and tore off chunks about the size of postage stamps.

"These'll make it a bit more comfy for you!" she whispered as she put them next to the van.

"Thanks, we'll be nice and cosy with these!" called Jane, as they gathered the soft sheets and pushed them between the open doors.

"See you later! I hope you can think of a way of getting us all to *Needle Crag* when it's light! Sleep well!"

With a last wave, they climbed into the van and shut the doors.

"Sleep well!" whispered Jamie, as he gently closed the drawer.

"We'll get you there alright! That's a promise!"

Merlyn, meanwhile, had circled the highest point of the crag three times, before gracefully descending to a rocky shelf just above the topmost branches of the trees below. With a flutter of his wings, he landed on the rough, weather worn rock and perched on the very edge.

The breeze ruffled his gleaming gold breast feathers as he waited for his passenger to alight from his carriage.

Lepho pushed at the wicker lid of the basket and then crawled out onto the stony cold ledge.

The breeze...a wind to him...immediately grasped at his purple cloak!

He pulled his hood over his head and shivered.

Shivered not only with the cold, but with the sights that filled his eyes!

Above him sat the enormous glowing owl, its own golden eyes watching his every move. But beyond the owl was an even more frightening sight! Below the vastness of the clear, starry sky lay a huge landscape lit silver by the moon. Lepho had never in his life witnessed such a sweeping expanse of moorland and forest stretching as far as his eyes could see.

The soaring caverns of *Aqua Crysta* seemed gigantic to him, the towering oak trees of the Harvest Lands even greater, but this...this size...this endless space, seemed incredible!

Together with the buffeting breeze, the sight made him feel dizzy and light-headed.

He felt himself swaying.

The owl, the stars, the distant horizon all began to swirl and whirl around him. He staggered, and then stumbled, perilously close to the edge of the rocky shelf!

His legs crumpled beneath him, and he fell against one of Merlyn's great ivory talons!

Then, with a last squinted glimpse of the whirling chaos that filled his giddy head, his eyes closed...

...and he knew no more...

As his eyes closed, the jay feather, blown by the breeze, loosened itself from the carriage basket and drifted away into the night air. Lepho's bringer of good fortune, gone with the wind...!

It was the very same wind from the south that greeted Mr Dawson at around six the next morning, as he stood in the porch doorway at the rear of *Deer Leap*. As he always did, come rain or shine, he stretched his arms skywards, took half-a-dozen deep breaths and then stretched downwards to touch his slippered toes.

As he strained to make his fingertips reach their goal, he noticed something unusual just beyond the grey stone porch step, nestled in the uncut grass.

A feather...a very unusual feather...(and not, if you're thinking it, Lepho's jay feather!)...a quill of such beauty and rarity, that he straightened his bent body with such speed that he nearly injured himself!

He groaned, clutched his waist muscles and then squatted in the doorway. Slowly, he reached for the feather and picked it up.

'A breast feather from an Eagle Owl??' he exclaimed to himself. 'But there are no Eagle Owls in this part of the World! Russia, yes. Finland, yes, but not the North Yorkshire Moors!'

"What's that, dad?" suddenly rang Jamie's voice from behind him.

The shock made Mr Dawson spring up into the air, once again nearly injuring himself!

"For goodness sake, Jamie, don't go creeping up behind folk at this time of the morning! I thought you'd still be in bed!" he gasped, clenching his middle again.

"I'm definitely beginning to think that something funny's going on!" he went on, inspecting the mottled brown, black and gold quill in his hand. "What, with the nightingale and the jay yesterday, then all the shenanigans in Jessica's bedroom last night...and now this! I just cannot understand it all!"

"Why, what is it?" Jamie repeated.

"This, my lad...oh, and by the way, happy birthday again, son...this, is a feather from an owl...an Eagle Owl, no less!"

58

Jamie stared at the quill with equal disbelief...but, as you can imagine, for different reasons!

"D...do you mean like...like the one we once saw in that bird-of-prey display back in Scotland a couple of years ago?" stumbled Jamie, trying to disguise his shock and avoid glancing up at Jessica's bedroom window.

"I do indeed!" said his father, shaking his head and turning into the kitchen.

"I just don't understand it! There can't be any Eagle Owls in North Yorkshire!"

"Perhaps it's escaped from a zoo or something!" said Jamie, trying his best to explain the mystery.

"Hmmm, that's a possibility, son," said his father, "I'll look into it." He put the feather on the kitchen table, next to a large box wrapped in brightly coloured paper.

"Do you want to open it now, or wait for your sister?" beamed Mr Dawson, in a more cheerful tone.

"No need to wait for me!" burst Jessica as she came into the kitchen in her dressing gown. "A girl can't get her beauty sleep with you two elephants clomping around! What's all the fuss about anyway?"

"Oh, never mind that now," insisted her father. "Let's concentrate on Jamie's birthday!"

So, with his dad and sister singing the 'Happy Birthday To You' song, Jamie began to open his cards and presents. The computer game from his sister was just the one he wanted.

"Thanks, sis!" he mumbled as he began to tear at the wrapping paper on the large box.

The singing continued, as the duet began an encore of the song.

"With that racket going on, I don't think we'll see that Eagle Ow...!" Jamie laughed.

"Jaammiee! What are you talking about!" Jessica gasped in a sort of musical sing-song voice, completely amazed that her brother had mentioned Merlyn.

Her dad, his rather flat singing having thankfully ground to a halt, picked up the feather and waved it in front of Jessica's nose.

"We reckon an Eagle Owl must have escaped from a zoo or something!" said Jamie quickly, winking madly at his sister.

Luckily, just at that moment, to distract everyone, Jamie tore off the last piece of wrapping paper, lifted the lid off the cardboard box and gazed open mouthed at what lay inside.

"Cor, dad, it's terrific!" he exclaimed, thrusting his hands into the box to lift out the wonderful gift. "Thanks a lot! It's fantastic!"

Gleaming brightly in the sunshine that was pouring through the kitchen window, the heavy model steam railway-engine, painted glossy black and green was, indeed, a splendid sight!

"It's the 'Clan Campbell'!" enthused Mr Dawson, who was train mad as a young boy. "A Standard Class Six, Pacific...number 72002! I spotted the real thing when I was about your age at Manchester Piccadilly!"

The engine, complete with green coal-tender with red trim, was about a foot and a half long, and perfect in every detail.

"You like it then, son?" Mr Dawson asked, lost in his own memories of the steam age.

"It's brill, dad!" smiled Jamie dreamily. "I just wish I could go on a real steam train someday!"

"Well!" beamed his father, sliding his glasses down his nose, and looking at Jamie with extra twinkly eyes, "that's the other surprise for your birthday! Have a look in the driver's cab!"

Folded tightly, among all the brass levers, wheels and dials, was a piece of cream paper. Jamie managed to poke his fingers into the cab and hurriedly fished it out. Then, excitedly, he unfolded it until the creased paper was fully open. He flattened it on his chest.

Written on it, in his dad's fancy handwriting that he used for special occasions, were the words:-

To Jamie, on your 10th birthday,

Three return tickets on the 7.30am train,
Saturday, May 1st.
from Goathland,
calling at Newtondale, Levisham and Pickering.

signed, Dad

Attached below by a paper clip were three small
tickets, with *"The North Yorkshire Moors Steam Railway"*
printed on each one.
When Jessica and Jamie read the word *'Newtondale'*, their minds
instantly imagined its deep gorge and *Needle Crag*! Thoughts of Lepho
and Merlyn, and then Jonathan and Jane upstairs in the top drawer
quickly flashed through their minds.
The tickets had suddenly become like gold-dust!
Jessica and Jamie looked at one another, and both smiled a knowing
smile.
The steam train would take them to Needle Crag!
And in only one hour from now!!

Chapter 8

"Wow, dad, that's brilliant!" burst Jamie, giving his father a hug.
"When are we going to set off to the station?"
Jessica and his father looked at him blankly.
They'd remembered what had happened in the forest the night before,
even if Jamie in his excitement hadn't.
"I'm sorry to say that there's a bit of a fly in the ointment, son,"
said his father, putting his arm round Jamie's shoulders. "We've no
transport!"
"And that means we can't get to the station in time!" sighed Jessica.
Jamie slumped down glumly onto a kitchen chair, looking very down in
the mouth! Not only wasn't his birthday treat going to be possible, but
the wonderful solution to their problem of getting to *Needle Crag* with
Jonathan and Jane had been well and truly scuppered!
"Curse those maniacs last night!" Jamie snapped, banging his fist on the
table.
"If it hadn't been for them, everything would be OK!"
        Mr Dawson, smiling quietly to himself, went over to
put the kettle on the range. Then, with his typical wicked sense of
humour, he suddenly burst into laughter.

"Do you want the *good* news...or the *bad* news?"

"The *good news*!, the *good news*!" replied Jamie, sitting up and wondering what was coming next.

His dad sat down next to him, still smiling broadly.

"Jim Murphy from Goathland Garage, will be here in exactly half-an-hour to take us to the station in his towing truck!"

Jamie, launched himself off his chair as though a firecracker had gone off under him! He whooped around the table once, then twice, and then suddenly stopped!

"What's the bad news?" he asked quietly, looking intently into his dad's face.

"The bad news is...that your wonderful, lovable, adoring father can't come with you on the train. I've got to sort out the Land Rover at Jim's garage, get all the shopping home and go to Whitby police-station to have a word about those deer poachers last night!"

"But dad, can't you...?" said Jamie sadly.

"No, no...my mind's made up! You and your sister can go by yourselves. After all, you're ten years old now and Jess is nearly twelve! I think you'll be OK! I'm sure you're quite capable of travelling to Pickering, having a look round and then catching a train back. Just ring me this afternoon and I'll pick you up at Goathland station! OK?"

Jessica and Jamie nodded, secretly relieved that their father wouldn't be going with them...but that two other tiny passengers would be! They could hardly wait to tell them the good news!

Meanwhile, far to the south, above the tangled, ancient trees that wrapped round the toes of *Needle Crag,* another tiny Aqua Crystan stirred from his deep sleep. His eyes flickered open and were dazzled by the brightness of the sun. He instinctively covered them with his cloaked arm, and then squinted at the blue sky.

For a moment or two he wondered where he was.

He certainly wasn't in his home town of Pillo! That was for sure!
There were no crystal studded walls, no bubbling River Floss, no
scrumptious fragrances in the air!

He sat up, gazed around and began to recall the
events of the night before. From his rocky ledge, he looked down on
the same vast landscape, now coloured in daylight with every shade
of green and brown. The sprawling heather lands stretched for miles,
merging in the far distance into the forest lands. Below, through the
knotted, gnarled branches he could make out the far side of a deep
valley, full of bright green ferns and young silver birch trees, and
threaded with a narrow, winding stream which glinted in the sun.
The dizzy height made him feel light-headed again, but at least the
breeze had vanished and the air was still and warm.

He suddenly remembered the flight beneath
Merlyn - the basket, the jay feather, the talons, the moving silvery
treetops through gaps in the wicker.
He shuddered at the thoughts and gazed high into the rocky crevices
of the crag that towered above him, to see if there were any signs of
the mighty bird.
But there were none.
The owl had obviously completed his task and disappeared.
What, pondered Lepho, was to happen next?

He walked away from the edge of the shelf towards
the sheer rock wall that had sprouted the ledge. It seemed similar to the
rock that made the stone walls of the Harvest Lands above *Aqua
Crysta*...orangy grey with patches of moss and pale green lichen.
Perhaps, in centuries past, rock had been quarried here and been used to
build the walls of the moorlands.
But then, as he moved his eyes towards the left, he noticed something
that made him gasp with astonishment!
He stopped and stared, unable to believe what he was seeing!
It was a window!

An arched window made from a mosaic of small,
multi-coloured, diamond shaped panes of glass held together with thin

strips of dark lead. It almost shimmered
in the bright sunshine, and, as he
stepped curiously towards it, each pane
seemed to change colour, as though the
window had a life of its own.
Its beauty and magic drew him
closer...and closer...

...until suddenly...

...he saw it...a shape...

...a face...staring back at him from beyond the glass mosaic!!

At exactly the same moment, Jessica and Jamies'
father was waving wildly through the railway carriage window, as the
7.30 steam train from Goathland hissed and chugged out of the station.
He ran with the rather smart, county cream and copper beech coloured
carriage until he reached the end of the short platform and then
disappeared from view.

"I bet he would have loved to have been with
us!" said Jessica, as she waved a last goodbye
and then delved into the side pocket of her
small rucksack.

"I've no doubt about it!" Jamie said,
stretching up to slide open the little
ventilation window. "But we both know that
it's a good job he couldn't!"

"I hope Jonathan
and Jane have
been OK in here,"
Jessica said. "It
was a pretty
bumpy journey in
Mr Murphy's
truck."

Carefully, she managed to lift the little *Ford 'T'* vintage van from the pocket and placed it on the window ledge. The two Aqua Crystans had loved sleeping in the van so much that they had decided it was the best way of carrying them to *Needle Crag*.

"Are you two alright?" she whispered into the tiny round windows at the back of the model.

The doors opened and Jonathan and Jane jumped out onto the narrow ledge.

"No problems at all!" called Jonathan, "but we're both glad to be able to stretch our legs! It's a bit cramped in there!"

They both ran along the wooden sill and then stared out of the window at the passing expanse of fields and moorland. Gradually, the train picked up speed, and the clicketty-click of the carriage wheels on the line became faster and faster.

"That sound takes me back to about the year *Nineteen-Fifty!*" shouted Jane above the din, "when our uncle once took us to Leeds on the train!"

Jessica and Jamie knelt on the rocking floor of their compartment, hoping that another passenger wouldn't suddenly come barging in from the corridor, and together, the four of them watched the sunlit scenery drift by.

It seemed so strange and magical to be with their tiny friends, travelling in an old railway carriage across the North Yorkshire Moors.

Suddenly, a loud noise from behind them nearly made everyone jump out of their skins! Jonathan and Jane dived back into the model van and shut the doors.

The compartment door slid open and there stood an elderly, white haired man in a grey waistcoat and grey trousers.

"Tickets, please!"

Jessica quickly stood up, fished out the tickets from the back pocket of her jeans, and handed them to the ticket-inspector. He clipped them and passed them back.

"Is it alright if we get off at the station in Newtondale?" Jamie asked.

"But you've booked all the way to Pick...!"

He suddenly stopped and stared at the window ledge.

Jessica and Jamie felt their hearts in their mouths again!

"That's a super model you've got there, kids!" the old man said. "It's a *Ford 'T'* if I'm not mistaken, isn't it? Can I have a look at it?"

As Jessica and Jamie held their breaths, the ticket-inspector stepped into the compartment.

"I used to drive one of these before the War...full size, of course!" he laughed. "Is it alright if I pick it up!"

It was too late to stop him!

He plucked the van from the ledge and inspected it as carefully as he inspected tickets.

"There you are!" he exclaimed, turning the model upside down. "It says *Ford 'T'* underneath!"

"Help! Help!" came a sudden squeaky cry from inside the van.

The ticket-inspector nearly dropped it with shock.

"I could have sworn I heard..!" he gasped, peering through the rear windows.

Just then, a young woman with a chubby baby in her arms appeared at the compartment doorway.

"Excuse me, could you tell me which way to the buffet-car?" she enquired.

The ticket-inspector turned, stared vacantly at the young woman, and then looked back at the upside down model.

"I...I...just heard it speak!" he said in a jerky, puzzled voice. "I..s..swear I just heard it s..speak!"

"Do you mind telling me where I can get a bite to eat!" snapped the woman, impatiently.

Calmly and slowly, the ticket-inspector inverted the van and placed it back on the window ledge. He then gathered his composure, adjusted his spotted bow-tie and walked into the corridor.

"This way, madam," he said, as he slid closed the compartment door and marched off with the young woman and baby behind him.

Jessica and Jamie quickly knelt on the floor by the window.

"Phew! That was a close one!" whispered Jessica. "Are you two alright?"

The back doors swung open and out stumbled a rather dishevelled pair of Aqua Crystans.

"I'm just glad we kept our soft tissue sheets in the van!" said Jane.

"Especially when he turned us upside down! What, with the rowing boat last night, and now the van, we're not having much luck with our transport!"

Luck seemed to have deserted the Mayor of Pillo, too...as he stared back into the face behind the rainbow window.

Through the diamond pane mosaic he could just make out a pair of aged, blue eyes set below an incredibly wrinkled brow and above a grim, thin lipped mouth. But it was the size of the face that worried Lepho more than anything! It was, as he expected, much, much larger than his own, but still only a fraction of those of his Upper World friends, Jessica and Jamie.

It was somewhere in between...like that of a doll to an Upper World person, but still that of a giant compared to him!

As he stared through the dancing panes, he also pondered whether or not this was the person who had sent the messages in the talons of Merlyn.

Was the face that of a friend or foe?

Bravely, thinking of Queen Venetia and Merrick, he ventured forward. After all, he had been *invited* here!

Just then, two bony hands appeared next to the face and pushed on the right-hand side of the window. Whoever it was, was trying to open it!

Slowly, half the window creaked open, gradually revealing more and more of the stranger's wizened face. Lepho had never seen such time-worn features in his life. He was used to seeing the Elders of *Aqua Crysta* such as Toby, Quentin and Merrick, but their faces looked like those of cherubs compared to the one that stared back at him now!

With half the window fully open, and still no trace of a welcoming word nor even a welcoming smile, Lepho wondered what to do next.

Perhaps he should say something!

Perhaps he...!

But then...the ancient face, without warning, suddenly sprung into life! A wide grin cracked across the pale, parched features and the blue eyes sparkled beneath the furrowed brow and completely hairless head.

The toothless smile seemed almost friendly.

Lepho stepped forward again, only to be stopped by a surprising gush of words!

"Greetings, my friend!" came a weak, croaky voice. "You must be the new Mayor of Pillo! We have been expecting you!"

"I am indeed Lepho, successor to Merrick in that honoured position," announced Lepho confidently. "I trust that you can lead me to his sisters, Hester and Gwenda!"

"I can, and will!" croaked the stranger. "Please, step this way! I am Grizel, butler and man-servant to the wise sisters."

Although Lepho still felt somehow worried and slightly suspicious about his welcome, he gingerly stepped forward towards the bony, sinewy hand that had now crawled down onto the rocky ledge followed by a green velvet clad arm. One of its long, deathly fingers, about the same height as Lepho, slowly beckoned him on, as the toothless grin widened across Grizel's face. Then...suddenly...like lightning...the hand pounced, and grabbed its prey in its clutches!

Lepho's shriek of anguish was unheard, as he was instantly deposited through the door of a brass lantern case that had appeared from nowhere. "Got you, my friend!" came Grizel's muffled cackle through the glass front of the lantern. "You're *mine*, all *mine*! To do with what I please!!"

Lepho's clenched fists hammered on the glass, but the more he did, the more his captor chuckled and laughed...and the more his eyes took on a look of anger and evil...

Chapter 9

Not far to the north, the steam train sped into the beginnings of Newtondale Gorge, its fern and heather clad sides soaring to meet the blue sky.

"We'll soon be there!" whispered Jessica to Jonathan and Jane, who were now sitting on the van's passenger seat gazing at the passing scenery from the window-sill.

There was a sudden volley of knocks on the glass panel of the compartment door, and the still rather bewildered face of the ticket-inspector mouthed the words,

'Next stop, Newtondale Halt!!'

Jessica gathered her rucksack, and Jamie carefully picked up the model van and put it in the breast pocket of his bright yellow T-shirt.

Still eyed by the curious inspector, they slid back the door and made their way along the rocking corridor, bumping from side to side.

When they reached the nearest carriage door, Jessica shoved down the

window and poked her head into the rushing wind. With her long, coppery hair streaming behind, she squinted into the Gorge.

Ahead, she could see the steam engine and the forward carriages rounding a bend in the line, grey and white smoke billowing from the engine's chimney.

A loud, shrill whistle sounded and echoed in the valley as the train began to slow and approach the deserted wooden strip of a platform.

As they waited for the train to stop, the inquisitive ticket-inspector hovered around behind them still unable to dismiss from his mind the sounds he had heard from the model van.

"You're having a walk in the gorge are you?" he enquired. "It's a lovely day for it!"

"Yes, we are," mumbled Jessica, wishing their inquisitor would take a walk himself down the corridor!

The train drew to a shuddering halt along side the platform and Jessica reached through the open window to twist the door handle. Once they were both off the train, Jamie banged the carriage door shut.

"Have a good day!" called the ticket-inspector. "Make sure you don't get lost!"

It was then that he had his second shock of the day.

"I wish you would!!" squeaked Jamie's T-shirt's breast pocket.

It was exactly the same voice the ticket-inspector had heard earlier!

His mouth dropped open in amazement. He was speechless.

As the train slowly chugged and hissed away from the platform, he stared at Jessica and Jamie as though he'd seen a ghost!

The gravelly path from the station wound along the bottom of the gorge for a while, before beginning to climb towards the rocky outcrops which crowned the deep valiey. Other than birdsong, all

72

was quiet in the sparse, silver birch woodland, with just the odd tall spruce or budded oak towering from the ferny undergrowth.

They rounded a bend, and more of the almost cliff-like, orangy grey outcrops came into view, still way above them.

Jamie stopped to catch his breath.

"That must be *Needle Crag*!" he gasped, pointing to the highest and sharpest peak.

"But how on earth are we going to get up there?" panted Jessica. "It's so high and we'll never get through all that undergrowth!"

"Can we have a look?" came Jane's tiny voice.

Jamie took the van from his shirt pocket and carefully put it on a large, flat rock by the side of the path. Jonathan and Jane, glad of a chance to stretch their legs, jumped down onto a patch of springy moss, and looked down into the gorge. It was already quite a distance down to the winding stream that wound along occasionally accompanied by a glint of railway track.

"I can see the platform as well!" pointed Jonathan. "I hope that nosy ticket-inspector has recovered from his shock!"

"Well it served him right for tipping us upside down!" laughed Jane. "It was so comfy in the back of the van until he came along!"

Just then, an orange-tip butterfly fluttered down from an overhanging fern and settled on the rock. With its white wings spread in the sunshine, it seemed totally unconcerned as Jonathan and Jane walked over to have a closer look.

Jessica and Jamie gazed, almost in disbelief, at the sight of two tiny people walking round a butterfly! It was one of those sights that made them feel like pinching themselves to check whether they were awake or not. It all seemed so fantastically magical!

"I wish we could jump on its back and fly!" beamed Jane, as she looked at the thousands of tiny overlapping scales that made up the wings, like tiles on a rooftop.

"Talking of flying," said Jonathan, stroking one of the orange-tip's twitching antennae, "I hope Lepho has arrived here safe and sound!"

"But how are we going to find him up there amongst all that lot?" said Jessica, looking at the tangle of undergrowth and gnarled, old tree branches that clothed the steepening side of the gorge.

"The magic will guide us, I'm sure!" said Jane. "If it's got us all this far then I'm sure it..."

"What was that?" Jamie burst suddenly. "I'm sure I heard something from up among those tree roots!"

They all looked up into the knotted stems, roots and branches just off their path.

"There it goes again! Listen!"

Lepho's faith in magical powers was beginning to dwindle as he clung on desperately to a candle stub inside the lantern. Through its glass front he could make out a seemingly never ending number of flickering candle flames coming into view and disappearing, and an endless rocky wall and wooden bannister spiralling downwards. Grizel was, indeed, descending an enclosed spiral stone staircase as fast as he could.

The lantern swung wildly from side to side as he climbed down each deep step, boring his way deeper into the depths of *Needle Crag*.

There were no more windows, the only light coming from the candles, which seemed to blur one into the next as Lepho jerkily watched through the thick glass.

Occasionally, Grizel would stop and rest, sitting on a step panting, and putting the lantern down beside him. It gave Lepho time to gather his breath, too, and wonder whether this journey was part of the great plan, or something else, something far more sinister.

Grizel's words '*to do with what I please*' kept ringing in his ears and taunting his imagination.

What did he mean? Where was he going?

Deeper and deeper, Grizel delved through the core of the crag, until at last, he stopped, much to Lepho's relief, by a large, arched wooden door, with a brass, circular handle.

Grizel put the lantern on the ground, reached on tiptoe to the handle and twisted it with both hands. The door, with an eerie creak, swung slowly open....

...and Lepho's eyes fell upon a sight that, at once, shocked him and chilled him to the bone!!

"It sounds like...like the *whinny of a horse!*" Jessica suggested, as all four listened.

"But surely, no one could ride a horse up here!" said Jonathan. "It's far too steep and overgrown!"

"There it goes again!" burst Jamie. "And it's getting closer!"

Without a doubt, the sound was that of a horse, yet it seemed close, and yet far away at the same time!

There was a sudden rustle from a patch of fern and bramble just above them. A thick, protruding tree root, covered in moss and lichen and lapped by dandelions, suddenly seemed to glow bright green in the sunshine.

And then...to the utter astonishment of Jessica, Jamie, Jonathan and Jane...the head and neck of a horse, a miniature horse, a chestnut horse with a black mane, no taller than a cocker spaniel...appeared from behind the tree root! Into the full glare of the sunshine it stepped, revealing loose, leather reins...and then the tiny hands and green velvet clad arms...of a *rider*!!

As Lepho stared through the thick glass of the lantern and beyond into the widening slice of murky light, he could just make out shelves upon shelves of ancient bottles. Bottles of every shape and size, some brown, some green, some clear. All were strewn with a centuries old, tangled mass of cobwebs and all were coated with a frost of dust.

But it was what was sitting beneath the shelves, slumped in an elaborately carved dark wood chair that sent wave after wave of shivers down his back!

A skeleton, an enormous human skeleton, complete in every detail from cranium to toe-bones, seemed to be guarding the ranks of bottles and their ancient contents!

It was as though a medieval apothecary or alchemist had died in his ancient store and never been moved since!

Tattered remnants of coarse, brownish cloth still clung to his rib-cage and leg bones, and an almost intact buckled leather belt girdled his hip bones in a loose, sagging loop!

Lepho gazed into the eyeless sockets of the bleached white skull which seemed to stare back at him, silently enquiring who was at the door!

Grizel cackled to himself, and then roughly grasped the lantern and entered the strange tomb. Candles flickered from rusty metal brackets fixed into the rocky walls, each casting jerkily moving shadows amongst the bottles. Faded, unreadable labels adorned every container naming their mysterious powdery or liquid contents. Bulbous glass stoppers sealed every one.

"Lucius will look after you until I return!" cackled Grizel, as he placed the brass lantern on a shelf between two green bottles.

Lepho banged his fists against the glass door of his prison.

"Take me to the sisters!" he bellowed as loudly as he could, a feeling of panic flowing through his body.

But Grizel took no notice.

Instead, he crept back towards the door.

Lepho fell to his knees in despair, and through moist eyes he watched his captor disappear and pull the heavy, arched door closed behind him. With a deafening clatter it shut fast, and Lepho was abandoned in the murky, flickering light, with the eerie remains of Lucius glowing beneath him.

Grizel's footsteps faded, together with Lepho's hope, as he put his head in his hands and quietly wept.

Meanwhile, in the hot, sweltering sunshine that fell upon the thick undergrowth beneath *Needle Crag*, the magical horse and its rider had emerged into their full glory.

Jessica, Jamie, Jane and Jonathan could hardly believe their eyes! As the chestnut horse swished its shining black tail and tossed its regal head, the miniature, doll-like rider...a woman...raised her green velvet clad arm and beckoned the children forward.

She was dressed from head to toe in a long, green cloak with black, leathery riding boots dangling from the hem - both at the one side of the horse. She was riding in the way of ladies from the past, side-saddle, with her delicate hands lightly holding the horse's leather reins.

Her face was mostly hidden by her long, wispy grey hair which flowed down her shimmering green velvet back.

Once more she beckoned gracefully, and then, for the first time, turned her head towards her watchers.

Jessica and Jamie gasped as her stare met their gaze.

The lady on the horse had a face that was the oldest imaginable! Wizened and lined, with eyes sunk into hollows, mouth thin and grim and nose long and hooked.

"She must be a witch!" whispered Jamie, unable to take his eyes away from the time worn face.

"Are we going to follow her?" whispered Jessica with a note of uncertainty in her voice.

"We *must* follow her!" insisted Jane from the flat rock. "She's part of the magic! She'll lead us to Merrick's sisters and to Lepho!"

The horse suddenly began impatiently padding the ground with one of its front hoofs.

"I agree!" said Jessica. "We've *got* to follow her. Come on then, you two, jump back in the van and let's get going!"

Jonathan and Jane scrambled into the *Ford 'T'* and Jamie gently closed the rear doors and carefully replaced the van into his shirt pocket.

Jessica lead the way off the path and towards the large tree-root, as the horse began to slowly trot into the undergrowth.

The way was steep and, although it was clear up to about knee level, the overhanging low branches of young trees made the going difficult for Jessica and Jamie.

It seemed so strange to be following the miniature horse and rider, which were almost like some kind of expensive battery driven toy. It was as though they ought to have a remote control to command its movements!

Onwards and upwards, the horse and rider climbed, occasionally disappearing from view, but always pausing to make sure that the two children were not left behind. The lady, whoever she was, seemed determined to lead Jessica and Jamie somewhere... *wherever that was*!

And, at the same time, her followers were also determined to keep up. Wherever somewhere was, they hoped, whenever they got there, they would find the authors of the mysterious messages.

The indistinct track, which was no wider than a couple of foot lengths, once or twice yielded signs that it had been wider and more prominent in the past.

Every so often, worn, old fence-posts protruded from the leafy grass, like soldiers guarding the path. Even one or two steps had to be climbed, or jumped in the case of the horse.

But eventually the track began to level off.

"We're almost at the foot of the cliff!" panted Jamie, as he pointed to the soaring wall of rock that loomed ahead, seemingly blocking the way. It was at this point that the lady slowly dismounted, and, still wordlessly, began to lead her horse to the left along a thankfully horizontal path.

Through the upper branches and budding twigs of the tallest trees Jessica and Jamie could see across the gorge and, when they dared, they could see the thin, winding thread of the stream far, far below, together with the glinting railway line.

They had certainly climbed a long, long way!

Indeed, both children were beginning to feel dizzy with the height and the exertion!

"How far have we to go?" ventured Jessica, hoping the green cloaked lady would speak. But she said nothing and just beckoned them onwards.

The path dipped and rose...and then, to Jessica and Jamies' relief, they saw ahead of them an opening in the sheer cliff face.

A black gash in the orangy grey rock...the entrance to a cave.

As they rounded a final bend, the full mouth of the black cave yawned before them....and there, standing in the shadows...was a figure!

The figure of a wizened old man with a toothless grin, and a completely bald head...the same size as the lady horse-rider and wearing a doublet of green velvet, wrinkled green leggings and sharply pointed black, leathery boots.

"Greetings!" he cackled, with a wave of his bony hand. "We have been expecting you! May I introduce myself? I'm butler and man servant to the wise sisters. Please step this way! My name is...*Grizel*!!"

79

Chapter 10

Through the bars of his cell which were his own fingers and beyond through the thick lantern glass, Lepho could make out the bounds of his confinement, distorted as they were by his tears of despair.

The dismal dungeon's candle flames danced to a sombre tuneless silence, as their pale light fell upon the ranks of bottles which not only lined the back wall of the cellar, but the side walls too, which swept round to the arched door. The ceiling and floor were both great expanses of rough, sandy rock. It seemed that the room had been carved from the solid rock beneath the *Needle*.

Although Lepho was thoroughly at home in the depths of the Earth back in *Aqua Crysta*, here he felt stifled by the mass of rock above him. He felt buried and trapped, and wondered whether he would ever see the light of day again.

And when his sad eyes fell upon the skeleton of the alchemist, he felt even more desperate. Just beyond the edge of the shelf was the enormous greyish white rib-cage with its great bony bars each as wide as Lepho himself and linked by the towering interlocking segments of the spinal column. This, in turn supported the vast dome of the skull, which, from behind, reminded him of a giant puff-ball fungus he had once come across on one of his Autumn food foraging expeditions into the Upper World.

He began to imagine the person whose skeleton it had been.

Lucius, the old alchemist in his brown cloak mixing magical potions from the contents of his countless bottles. His long fingers grasping glass flasks and swishing colourful powders and liquids together to conjure up all manner of remedies and spells. His face, white whiskered and bearded with hooked nose and bright eyes, poring over the chemicals and cackling magical, mystic rhymes to himself.

Perhaps he had been a sage or a wizard of great renown and celebrated throughout the Land.

Lepho wished for his magic to help him now...but he knew that he was helpless.

Escape was impossible.

He was at the mercy and whim of that other cackling creature...Grizel. Would he ever come back? And, if he did, what were his plans?

Grizel, however, at that moment, was concerned with his other visitors.

"Follow me into the cave!" he called from the shadows, and Jessica and Jamie stepped forward out of the bright sunlight and into the gloom.

They could see that their host was about the same size as the lady horse-rider, no taller than their knees, and when they were together, they could see their facial resemblance. Both had the same wrinkled brows, sunken blue eyes and angular chins.

"You have met my sister, Grizelda!" Grizel called as the two of them turned and walked into the depths of the cave.

"I apologise for her lack of welcoming words but she has long since lost the power of speech!" he cackled. "I shall have to do all the talking until you meet the wise sisters!"

Jessica thought that she had better say something and try to strike up some kind of friendship. After all, they were there to help save *Aqua Crysta*...and these two strange characters were presumably part of whatever lay ahead!

"Thankyou for inviting us!" she muttered. "Have you met our friend Lepho, the new Mayor of Pillo, the township of *Aqua Crysta*?"
Grizel turned and put his bony hand to his ear.
"What is that you say? Speak up!" he cackled. "My sister has lost her voice, but I, I'm afraid, am losing my hearing!"
Grizelda, who was leading the horse, made some signals to her brother with her free hand as Jessica repeated her question a little more loudly.
"Have you met...?"
"Ah, Lepho, you mean?" burst Grizel, having understood his sister's signals.
"No, he hasn't arrived yet!"
"But, the owl Merlyn must have reached here by now, surely?" called Jessica with a note of alarm in her voice.
"Merlyn, I'm afraid, often has a mind of his own!" said the wizened dwarf, with a shrug of his shoulders. "He may be here, he may be there! Who knows? Let's just hope he arrives in time!"
"In time for what?" gasped Jamie, a little impatiently.
"In time to save your friend's realm of *Aqua Crysta*, of course! Its end is nigh!"
Jessica and Jamie both began to fear for Lepho's safety!
Perhaps he was miles away and lost...or worse!
Perhaps the owl had taken him to some perch or nest nowhere near the *Needle*!
They were beginning to doubt the magic that had lured them to this faraway cliff.
"Then please take us to Hester and Gwenda as quickly as you can!" demanded Jessica in as bold a voice as she could muster.
"It was they who wrote the messages. Perhaps Lepho is already with them!"
"I think not!" muttered Grizel, almost under his breath.
"What was that you said?" called Jamie, who was becoming increasingly annoyed by Grizel's manner.

"Yes, yes, I think *so!*" he cackled back accompanied by his toothless grin.

Jessica and Jamie looked at one another, both having taken a dislike to their host...but for the moment they would follow him and his silent sister and hope that their distrust was unfounded.

Grizel, Grizelda and her horse lead them deeper and deeper into the cave, leaving the bright sunlight far behind. The cave floor sloped gently downwards and the roof gradually became lower and lower until Jessica and Jamie had to slightly stoop forwards to avoid banging their heads!

Fortunately the roof didn't get any lower, but as they walked along they began to notice strange objects littering the floor at each side. By now candle brackets on the walls lit the way, and Jessica and Jamie couldn't help pointing to the most unexpected of items!

Old fashioned circular birdcages, brass coal scuttles, pokers, copper kettles, floral teapots, dusty leather-bound books, gilt framed oil paintings of splendid country mansions and rosy cheeked young ladies, elegant water jugs decorated with Chinese garden scenes...and many, many more objects...all lining the cave like some strange, secret, underground antiques warehouse!

It was most peculiar, and at one point the antiques were piled so high and wide that it was a bit of a squeeze to get through!

But onwards they went until Jessica and Jamie began to hear the sound of bubbling, gurgling water and could make out a golden glow of light in the distance.

Suddenly, Grizel and Grizelda stopped by a carelessly piled heap of violins, all looking like huge double basses or cellos next to the dwarfs. Both of them were silhouetted against the bright golden light and beyond Jessica and Jamie could see the cave beginning to swell into more of a low roofed but very wide cavern.

"No one from the Outside World has set eyes upon our realm for over two centuries!" cackled Grizel. "So consider yourselves honoured!"

He and his sister stepped forward into the warm, glowing brilliance, followed by their amazed visitors.

Before them, amid hundreds of flickering candles, was a perfectly round pool of golden water surrounded by a low marble wall. In the middle was a single, gushing fountain spouting more golden water up to a height about that of Jamie. The tinkling sound it made was at once comforting and welcoming.

"It's beautiful!" whispered Jessica as she walked towards it, in awe of its gentle splendour.

"These must be the *Golden Waters of Needle Crag* that Lepho told us about," whispered Jamie, slowly kneeling by the low wall.

"People came in their hundreds and thousands over the years to sample the magic," explained Grizel in a slightly more friendly voice, "until Hester and Gwenda grew tired."

Jamie reached into his shirt pocket and carefully placed the *Ford 'T'* on the top of the smooth wall.

"Have a look at this!" he whispered as he opened the rear doors. Jonathan and Jane climbed down and they, too, were enchanted by the vast golden lake that stretched before them, crowned by the enormous glittering fountain.

It was at that moment that Grizel suddenly noticed the two visitors he hadn't been expecting.

His mood seemed to change in an instant as he thought of his other Aqua

Crystan captive up in the alchemist's room, but he tried his best to conceal his delight.

"Ah, ah! Aqua Crystans I dare say!" he cackled, with a forced toothless smile.

"May I also welcome *you* to our realm!"

"Thankyou, sir!" replied Jane. "This is my brother Jonathan and I'm Jane!"

Grizel would have liked, then and there, to have grabbed the tiny Aqua Crystans and imprison them with their compatriot, Lepho, but he realised that he would be no match for Jessica and Jamie. He would have to wait for an opportunity.

"Why is the cave back there full of antiques?" asked Jessica.

Grizel, while still gazing at Jonathan and Jane, snapped, "They may be antiques to you, my dear, but for us they were welcome payment!"

"Payment for what?" queried Jamie.

Grizel diverted his eyes from his prey and resumed his friendlier tone.

"Payment for sampling our *Golden Waters*! Money was of little use to us here, so people would bring an item or two of worth in exchange for a drop or two of our magic. The word soon got around in the Outside World that the water had properties that cured illnesses and gave eternal youth! Day after day, Hester and Gwenda would sit here on the wall of the *Golden Pool* and accept gifts of food, drink and the artifacts you have seen. There are even more by the *Golden Lagoon* as you will shortly see for yourselves!"

Grizel once again eyed Jonathan and Jane with a look of sinister desire, but thoughts of a *Golden Lagoon* made Jessica even more inquisitive and she distracted the dwarf for a second time.

"Lepho told us that Hester and Gwenda eventually stopped dispensing the *Golden Waters*!"

Grizel forced himself to smile again.

"That is correct! In Georgian times the whole circus just became too much! Even more and more people began to arrive! Queues of visitors would stretch way beyond the mouth of the cave...but things began to get even worse when Hester, Gwenda and the rest of us began to be looked upon as *freaks*! Not only did we appear to be very young for our advancing years...!"

Grizel's voice suddenly dropped and became reflectively sad.

"...but we also began to lose our stature!...our size!...our height!"

For the first time, the four visitors began to feel some sympathy for their hosts.

Grizel continued, with a hint of anger mixed with regret tainting his voice.

"Some of us were even forcibly taken...kidnapped from our world...and put into freak shows in Georgian towns and cities in the Outside World!"

He looked at his sister with unusually sorrowful eyes.

"Our own mother, father and older sisters were taken! We never saw them again! We learned that they had been exhibited in London...*in cages!...poked fun at!...forced to dance and entertain people at fairs!*...our sisters were even sold to become the freakish 'pets' of a close relative of King George the Third himself!!"

He sat down on the marble wall crushed by his memories.

Grizelda comforted him, and the children felt pangs of guilt for what Upper World folk had got up to in the dim and distant past.

A moment or two of silence passed, before Grizel suddenly jumped up from the wall and paced up and down with his head bowed.

Then, abruptly, the silence was shattered!

"I just *cannot* do it!" he exclaimed. "I *cannot* bring myself to do it!"

Jessica, Jamie, Jonathan and Jane looked at one another wondering what on earth was coming next!

"Do *what*? What are you talking about?" ventured Jamie, somewhat puzzled.

Grizel looked up into the eyes of his larger visitors and then cast his eyes down towards the tiny Jonathan and Jane.

He spoke slowly and solemnly.

"I *cannot*...! I just *cannot* put you through the same hell as my long lost relatives and friends!"

"What do you mean?" asked Jessica, even more puzzled.

"Let me tell you the truth," said Grizel, "but please promise me that you will not be angered by what you hear!"

"We promise, we promise...but what have you got to say? Please tell us!" Jessica pleaded.

Grizel took a deep breath...and began his tale.

Chapter 11

It was more of a confession than a tale that Grizel began to relate as he paced slowly between his sister's horse and the low circular wall which surrounded the pool. His four visitors listened intently and became more and more shocked by the dwarf's revelations of how Merlyn had arrived back at the *Crag* as expected, but then the Mayor of Pillo had fallen headlong into Grizel's wicked plans.

Grizel told of how he had decided that he would profit by the Upper World's desire to encounter the freakish. He would somehow sell Lepho to the Outside World for whatever sum he demanded.

Lepho would be put on show in a cage or a bottle and people would come from far and wide to see the two inch high figure.

Grizel would become wealthy and Lepho would be celebrated throughout the Upper World!

Grizel's audience listened with horror at what had hatched in the dwarf's mind. Jessica and Jamie thought of what the consequences would be in the modern World - newspaper and television tycoons bidding for exclusive rights to reveal the '*Find of the Century*', examinations in scientific laboratories, not to mention the torment that Lepho would have to endure and the probable result that...*Aqua Crysta* itself would be discovered!!

"So we must release your friend Lepho as soon as possible!" concluded Grizel, "and we must proceed with your *Quest to save Aqua Crysta*!!"

"Then tell us where you have imprisoned him!" said Jessica at last. "We must rescue him immediately! Time is running out!"

"You are not angry with me?" asked Grizel guiltily.

"It's no use being *angry*!" said Jamie as calmly as he could. "You have realised your mistake in the nick of time. The important thing is to find Lepho and get on with our mission. Take us to him!"

Grizel, with a certain amount of relief, made his way to the far side of the pool and beckoned to the children to follow. He watched as Jonathan and Jane jumped back into the van and Jamie replaced it in his shirt pocket. As Jessica and Jamie skirted round the pool carefully avoiding the myriad of candles, Grizelda mounted her horse and trotted away further into the cavern.

"I wonder where *she's* going," whispered Jamie.

"Probably back to Hester and Gwenda, wherever they are!" replied Jessica.

Meanwhile Grizel headed fairly quickly towards the right-hand wall of the cavern where the outline of an arched doorway could soon be seen. As they all approached it, Jessica and Jamie could make out the beginnings of a staircase carved into the rock.

Grizel turned and beckoned once more, and soon all three were climbing the steep steps, lit by regular candle brackets.

The steps began to spiral more and more sharply, and although Jessica and Jamie found the height of each step comfortable, their leader was finding them quite a climb!

"The stairs were obviously built for taller people!" whispered Jamie, watching

Grizel struggle. Jessica almost felt like helping him, but she still had a disliking for him, especially after having heard the goings on in his mind!

"Remember he was much taller once," she whispered. "I wonder if the shrinking is anything to do with the *Golden Water*. Is it similar, but less powerful than the bubbling waters of *Aqua Crysta*?"

"Well I think there must be some sort of connection between here and *Aqua Crysta*!" suggested Jamie. "In both places folk live for centuries, but here they become smaller slowly, whereas in *Aqua Crysta* just leaping down from the well makes you tiny!"

After about thirty steps Grizel suddenly stopped and produced an enormous iron key from a ledge.

"Oh, I don't need this!" he muttered, absent-mindedly. "I didn't lock him in!"

He then pointed to the arched wooden door with the circular handle. Jamie rushed forward, turned the handle and pushed open the door. The sight of what faced him made him recoil with horror and cover his eyes!

"It's alright, Lucius can do you no harm," cackled Grizel. "He died years ago!"

Jessica cautiously peered into the room behind her brother and gasped when she saw the skeleton staring back at her. She almost screamed at the gruesome sight, but thoughts of finding Lepho stifled her.

"Where is he?" Jamie demanded, his eyes scanning the shelves of bottles and cobwebs.

"Just move into the room and you will see him in a lantern behind Lucius," cackled Grizel.

Jessica and Jamie tentatively and nervously stepped further into the strange room...

...and then it happened!!...

...so quickly, they didn't know what had hit them!

"Lucius can't harm you, but *I certainly can*!!" cackled Grizel in a frenzy of sudden movement.

In a flash he'd darted out of the door, slammed it shut and locked it! Jessica and Jamie pushed and shoved the wooden door with all their might but it was useless. They were well and truly trapped. Tricked by the nasty, evil dwarf!

They sank to the rocky floor and then heard their captor's faint cackling coming through the door.

"That's *three* Aqua Crystans to sell! A very good day's work! A very good day's work, indeed!"....followed by fading cackling laughter as Grizel disappeared down the steps!

"*Let us out! Let us out!*" called Jamie in vain, as he banged the door with a clenched fist. "Open this door in the name of Queen Ven...!!" But he knew it was useless.

Grizel had gone and they were left imprisoned in this hideous cell!

Silently, they looked around their dungeon. The rows of dusty bottles festooned with hammocky cobwebs, the flickering, eerie candles and, worst of all, the slumped skeleton of Lucius like some kind of horrific guard!

"Now what do we do?" sighed Jamie, reaching into his pocket for Jonathan and Jane.

He got to his feet and put the *Ford 'T'* on the palm of his hand.

"I'm sorry about this, folks, but I'm afraid we've let you down again!" he whispered into the front of the van.

Jonathan and Jane pushed open the back door and jumped onto his hand.

"Don't worry, we'll soon be out of this little pickle!" smiled Jane confidently.

"We've been in tighter spots than this! The magic will still be with us I'm sure!"

It was then that Jessica spotted the brass lantern behind the skull of Lucius. There was a tiny figure slumped by the flameless, stubby candle in the middle. It was Lepho.

"Lepho, Lepho, are you alright?" she shouted, her face almost touching the lantern's thick glass.

The tiny figure didn't stir, so Jessica anxiously tapped on the glass. With that, Lepho slowly opened his eyes and looked with a mixture of sudden alarm and then relief at the huge face before him, grotesquely contorted by the glass.

He rushed over to his transparent prison wall and mouthed a silent *"Let me out!"*

Jessica's fingers searched for a latch on the door and eventually the glass panel sprung open and Lepho leapt out onto the dust coated shelf.

"Thank goodness I'm out of there!" he gasped. "I thought I would never be free again! But how did you two get here? Are Jonathan and Jane with you?"

"We are!!" they called as Jamie lowered them to the shelf allowing them to join the Mayor of Pillo.

"We were tricked by Grizel into thinking we were going to rescue you, but instead we've *all* been captured!" said Jonathan.

"Don't worry!" beamed Lepho. "He's no match for us! We'll be out in no time, but we've got to act quickly before he returns!"

"But he's locked us in!" sighed Jessica.

"Ah, but he didn't take into account the cunning of we Aqua Crystans!" said Lepho with a twinkle in his eye. "See the gap under the door?"

"You mean you three are just going to *walk out*?" burst Jamie with a smile that suddenly faded. "But what about *us*?"

"The *key*, the *key*, of course!" exclaimed Jessica. "If it's still on the ledge outside then...!"

"But three Aqua Crystans will never be able to move it! It's huge!" said Jamie.

"And besides, he may have taken it with him!"

"First things first!" insisted Lepho. "Lift me up to the keyhole and let me have a look to see if it's there!"

A moment later, with the help of Jessica, Lepho was making his way easily through the keyhole. Once at the far side he carefully held onto the sides as he peered down to the small landing just outside the door.

Jessica put her eye to the hole and could see the tiny figure of Lepho silhouetted against the candlelight of the staircase.

"Can you see the key?" she whispered. "It should be on a ledge next to the last step!"

"Yes, yes...it's there!"called back Lepho. "But you're right! It's enormous!"

He dashed back through the hole and jumped onto Jessica's hand.

"We'll never be able to move it!" he sighed.

Hope of escape was suddenly shattered!

So near and yet so far, the key was so frustratingly close!

A glum silence fell upon them all as they racked their brains trying to think of a way of somehow getting the key to the lock. It was Lucius who had the answer!

His hollow stare was fixed on the solution, and luckily it was Jonathan's eyes that, by chance, happened to fall upon the same object on the floor by the door...a pot of wax-coated tapers for lighting candles!

"I've got it!" he exclaimed, almost causing the rest of the captives to jump out of their skins! "All we've got to do is to take the strings out of those wax tapers and tie them together, then..."

"...We make a long chain and tie one end to the key...!" burst Jane.

"...And pull it through the gap under the door...!" added Jessica excitedly.

"...And *bingo*! We're *free*!!" finished Jamie.

In next to no time, Jessica and Jamie had expertly picked off the wax at each end of all

ten tapers and had knotted them together to make a lengthy chain.
They then put Lepho, Jonathan and Jane on the floor and a moment later
the tiny trio were dragging the chain across the landing towards the
ledge. Quickly they tied the string to the key, rushed back and appeared
under the door.

"Keep your fingers crossed!" called Jamie, as he gently pulled on his
end of the chain.

They heard a faint clatter as the key was nudged off the ledge.

Jamie paused, hoping the knot hadn't undone...or, even worse...Grizel
had heard the noise!

He pulled again...but disaster struck!

Jamie toppled backwards into his sister who all but fell into the bony
arms of Lucius!

The knot had broken!

More valuable time would have to be spent by the Aqua Crystans
dragging the string over to the key, and they all knew that Grizel could
return at any moment!

Nevertheless the risk was worth taking!

It had to be taken!

The tiny trio once again scampered under the huge
door, scurried across the rocky landing and tied the string as tightly as
they could to the key. When they returned, Jamie, heart in his mouth,
gently tugged...and this time he could sense the precious key sliding
across the landing!

On and on it went...

...and then...

...it suddenly stopped...stuck fast!!

"What's the matter this time?" he gasped.

Lepho dashed under the door to see what had happened...and what he
saw made his heart sink!

An enormous black leather boot lay straddled across the string chain
clamping it to the floor...and then a frail, pale, sinewy hand at the end of
a green velvet arm appeared from above...and grasped the key!

Terrified, he rushed back to the others!

"Grizel's back!" he exclaimed in as loud a voice as he could.

In the anxious silence that followed, all the prisoners wondered what was going to happen next.

"What's that?" Jonathan squeaked from the floor of the cell.

A noise was coming from the keyhole!

The key was being pushed in jerkily and uncertainly.

Then it was being turned.

The lock's mechanism clattered in the silence as all eyes were fixed on the keyhole!

"Quickly, Jess!" whispered Jamie. "Get behind the door so we can pounce on him!"

Both of them flattened themselves against the shelves by the door waiting for their evil captor to enter.

The arched door began to slowly open with an eerie creak...

Jessica and Jamie held their breaths...their hands, fingers clawed, ready to grab the villainous Grizel.

Wider and wider the door creaked open... and then...

...the tip of a black, leathery boot appeared...

Chapter 12

"NOW!!" yelled Jamie, as he grabbed the edge of the door and yanked it open.

In a flurry of arms and legs he and his sister pounced on the knee high figure that straddled the threshold.

The green clad dwarf, cowered and raised protective arms against the two giants...and then...as quickly as they had begun their attack, Jessica and Jamie stopped, and looked at their captive in astonishment!

It wasn't Grizel at all!

It was his sister, *Grizelda*!

Quivering with fright and her sad, hollow eyes gazing up at them fearfully, she silently pleaded with Jessica and Jamie to follow her out of the room.

She beckoned wildly with her arms and made for the spiral staircase.

"It could be another trick!" whispered Jamie suspiciously.

"I don't think so," replied Jessica. "I think she's on our side and wants us to meet Hester and Gwenda as quickly as possible! Come on, let's follow her!"

Jamie gathered Jonathan, Jane and Lepho into the *Ford 'T'* and tucked the van into his shirt pocket. As he darted out of the room after his sister and Grizelda, he glanced back at the skeleton.

"Sorry we couldn't stay for a chat, Lucius, but we've important business to attend to!" he called with a smile, as he closed the door.

At the bottom of the stairs, Grizelda untethered her chestnut horse and quickly mounted her. A moment later she was galloping across the floor of the low cavern past the golden fountain, avoiding even more scattered piles of antiques. Jessica and Jamie followed as quickly as they could, as the candle light began to fade away from the pond.
Once or twice, Grizelda disappeared from view, but she kept stopping to make sure she was still being followed.

At the far end of the cavern where the ceiling became even lower, she stopped, dismounted and opened another arched wooden door. It towered above her, and she needed a panting Jessica to help her open it. As the door slowly opened a bright familiar light flooded out from beyond and illuminated the astonished faces of Jessica and Jamie.
"It *can't be!*" gasped Jessica as she gazed through the doorway.
"It *can't be!*"
"*Aqua Crysta!!*" exclaimed Jamie, as he too stared at what lay beyond the door.
"But we're *miles* away!" Jessica panted. "It's *impossible!*"

Before them was an enormous cavern, its pink and white rocky walls dotted with thousands of light giving crystals! As they stepped into the awesome splendour, their eyes were filled with the beauty all around them. They had stepped from one low, gloomy cavern into one of such magnificence that it almost took their breaths away! The high roof was packed with glistening pink stalactites...just like *Aqua Crysta*...but it was what lay in front of them that amazed them even more!
Stretching for as far as their eyes could see was a vast, wide shimmering mirror, reflecting the forest of stalactites above it and doubling the light from the crystal studded walls.

It was a lake, so smooth that not a single ripple could be seen. In fact, if it hadn't been for the gentlest of lapping wavelets on its shore, it could have been made of the purest glass!

The narrow shore which swept round in each direction from the door was dazzlingly white, like a coral beach!

Jessica knelt down and sifted the sugary sand between her fingers.

"It's crystal sand!" she whispered. "It's beautiful! I could stay here for ever!"

But, as Jamie rightly pointed out, there was no time for dawdling, nor staring at the scenery!

There was business to be done!

There wasn't even time for the three Aqua Crystans to have a peep at this wondrous cavern and be reminded of home!

Time was of the essence and already Grizelda had mounted her horse and was heading along the shore to the left, the chestnut mare's hoofs sinking into its sugary sand.

Other than the soft padding of hoofs and the merest tinkle of breaking wavelets, the cavern was eerily silent. There was no sign of Grizel, although the children kept expecting him to suddenly appear from the shadows and somehow delay their quest. On and on they went round the seemingly endless shore, until gradually they began to make out large, angular silhouettes in the distance.

As they approached them, they began to realise that the shapes were those of old fashioned Queen Anne chairs, dressers, tables, writing desks and even hat stands bedecked with velvet cloaks and ladies' headwear decorated with long bird plumes. It was most peculiar.

It was like entering an historic stately home...yet underground, in a cavern with a lake! Very peculiar, indeed!

Then they began to hear the soft sound of music...like a piano, but not a piano...more like a harpsichord with plucked strings instead of hammered ones.

As they made their way between the ornately carved, dark wood furniture, the notes became louder and louder, echoing across the shimmering vastness of the lake.

Gilt framed paintings and great mirrors, without a hint of tarnish hung from the pinky white cavern walls. And, just beyond an elegant dresser dripping with silver plates, dishes, gravy boats and goblets, was a magnificently long tapestry depicting an English country scene of long ago.

It was as fresh and as vibrant as the day it had been completed.

Skilful fingers had sewn a perfect landscape of forest and hills with roaming stags, wild boar, a winding river valley, a thatched village, a distant castle and golden eagles soaring in the sky.

The music by now was so strident and lively it seemed they were surrounded by swirling notes played by even more skilful fingers.

The air was filled with melody...and then, Jessica's eyes fell upon the largest piece of furniture of all...a bed, a four-poster bed, draped in fine, billowing swathes of gold cloth, its feet sunk into the crystal sand, two of them almost lapped by the lake's gentle, silver wavelets.

Grizelda came to a halt. She dismounted and tethered the mare to the chunky leg of a small but heavy wooden table. The table held a golden tray laden with a delicate, floral tea-set fashioned from bone china.
The music stopped.
Grizelda beckoned the guests and smiled a toothless smile similar to her brother's.

Jessica and Jamie nervously stepped forward...and then, from just beyond the golden drapes appeared a figure...

...a bent, fragile figure...as fragile as the bone china on the tea tray...

...the figure of an old, old lady, smaller than Grizelda, but equally grey, wizened and wrinkled.

Grizelda curtseyed to her mistress, glanced back and waved a welcoming hand to Jessica and Jamie.

The lady, in her long, red velvet gown, smiled and spoke in a voice just loud enough to be heard above the gentle lapping of the lake.

"Our honoured guests, I presume!"

Jessica, wondering what on earth to say, nodded and smiled.

"I am Hester, long lost sister of Merrick, recently deceased Mayor of Pillo. Thankyou for making the journey. Come and meet my twin, Gwenda... but step slowly, for she is close to death."

Jessica and Jamie tiptoed round the end of the enormous bed taking care not to step into the shallow water. At the other side they saw the harpsichord with a ladder propped up to the keys and then they nervously looked through a gap in the golden drapes.

There, lying at their side of the bed, was the sleeping Gwenda, her face, the mirror image of her sister, pale, lined and hollow cheeked. She was like a china doll, frail and silent, with just the shallowest of breathing indicating she was alive...her thin, wispy grey hair flowing over the golden pillow.

"A cup of cold tea for our guests, Grizelda," said Hester, "while I explain what has to be done."

Grizelda obediently busied herself preparing the refreshments, while Jessica and Jamie knelt in the crystal sand by the bed. Hester asked to be lifted onto the bed and Jessica carefully obliged. As she gently picked her up by the waist, she was amazed by the lightness of the doll-like figure in her hands and was anxious that she didn't squeeze her too much. She seemed so fragile, that she might crumble to dust at any moment!

Gently she sat her on the edge of the golden bed.

From the other side of the four-poster bed they could hear the shrill tinkle of china and dribbling tea as Grizelda filled the dainty cups from the small floral pot. A second or two later she dutifully appeared with one cup and saucer and then she scurried back for the second.

Each cup looked like a large soup bowl in her tiny hands, but they were, in fact, so small in the hands of Jessica and Jamie, that there couldn't have been more than half a dozen sips of the dark, milkless brew in each one!

Nevertheless, they politely sipped the cold liquid and tried desperately to keep their faces straight as they tasted the bitter, and presumably, ancient tea!

As a welcome diversion, Jamie placed his cup and saucer on the bed and carefully lifted the *Ford 'T'* from his pocket and opened the rear doors. Jonathan and Jane jumped onto his palm followed by Lepho.

"The Mayor of Pillo?" enquired Hester, as she gazed with interest at the trio.

"Correct, madam!" said Lepho. "And these are two of my compatriots from the realm of *Aqua Crysta*, Jonathan and Jane. But can I first of all, on behalf of Queen Venetia, offer our regrets concerning the passing away of your brother, Merrick?"

"You may, and I am grateful for your words," replied Hester. "Although we went our separate ways over three centuries ago, my sister and I have always kept him in our hearts. But it is the matter of his death and, as you can see, the closeness to death of our sister, Gwenda, that compelled me to summon you here!"

She paused and looked at her sister sadly.

"Somehow we have to travel away from the *Golden Waters* and make *Aqua Crysta* our destination. My sister must be reunited with Merrick in death on the *Island of Avalon* which lies near *Old Soulsyke*. There is still hope for me to remain alive within the powerful magic of your realm. For, as long as one of us lives then your land is safe and all those who dwell there. We must depart as soon as we can!"

"Who shall make the journey, my lady?" asked Lepho.

"Myself, Gwenda and our two servants, Grizelda and her brother...we will endure the hardships ahead somehow...though it is going to be difficult for my sister! You can see how frail she is!"

"But is your butler, Grizel, to be trusted?" asked Lepho anxiously. "We have already encountered his evil plots!"

Hester knowingly smiled.

"Grizel and his sister are, along with us, the last survivors of the *Realm of the Golden Waters*. They have been our companions and servants for centuries. Grizel's mind is weak but he means no har...."

"But he schemed to capture these Aqua Crystans and sell them to the Outside World...to make his fortune...and put the whole of their magic kingdom at risk!" burst Jessica, unable to contain herself.

"I know of his anger concerning the way in which his family were stolen and mistreated in the time of King George, two centuries ago, but, believe me, he is harmless. He could *never* have carried out what he planned. His mind was running away with itself! It often does!" Grizelda nodded and smiled.

"Well if you are sure, then we must make haste!" said Lepho. "What is your plan?"

"There's just one thing I don't understand," interrupted Jamie. "What is your concern?" asked Hester.

"The '*Lights*'! The '*Lights from the Skies*'!", replied Jamie, wondering whether or not he should have mentioned them at all. "The ones you wrote about in your message!"

Hester first looked down at the three Aqua Crystans and then looked at both Jessica and Jamie. She clenched her hands together making a knot of her frail white fingers and knuckles. They reminded Jamie of the skeletal hands of Lucius back in the alchemist's room.

She took a deep breath and it seemed that whatever she had to say was going to be difficult for her.

"I will tell you once we set sail!" she eventually said, somehow relieved that she didn't have to relate the tale just yet. "We have no time to lose. By the time we reach the far side of the lake you shall know all there is to know!"

"Set *sail?*" Jessica burst, shocked by Hester's words. She had presumed that they would be returning the way they had come.

"It is the quickest and smoothest way for my sister!" said Hester. "Although when I say '*set sail*' it is slightly misleading!"

She pointed along the shore.

Moored just a little further along the crystal sands with a sagging rope trapped in a closed dark wood chest, was a boat...a rowing boat.

"This is the reason we need *your* help," said Hester to Jessica and Jamie. "For we are now too small and weak to row across the lake. Once we could have made the voyage, but now we require strength from the Outside World, not only for this part of the journey but also for the rest of way to the *Island of Avalon* and *Aqua Crysta*. This is why the magic has brought you here!"

Jessica and Jamie looked at one another and both immediately realised what the other was thinking, as did Lepho, Jonathan and Jane. For all of them, memories flooded back of the little red rowing boat that the Gargoyle, Dodo, had taken from the beach at Sandsend during their adventure of Christmas Eve. The boat in which

they had travelled through the *Cave of Torrents* and returned the Magwitches to *Torrent Lodge*. The boat that had just last night been used to ferry Merrick across to his resting place on the *Island of Avalon*...and then been crushed into splinters under the wheels of the poachers' pick-up truck!

Sad memories, however, were quickly dispelled, as Hester began to busily prepare her sister for the journey. Jessica helped and in no time she was making her way along the shore with the still sleeping Gwenda cradled in her arms, wrapped securely in a golden sheet from the bed.

Behind her came Jamie with the Aqua Crystans safely back in the *Ford 'T'* nestled snugly in his shirt pocket. Then came Grizelda arm in arm with the bent figure of Hester and leading her beloved chestnut mare. The only person missing was Grizel, but Grizelda felt sure he would appear soon...and, indeed, it wasn't long before he *did* appear...

...but not *quite* in the way any of them expected!!

Chapter 13

It was Jessica who noticed him first as he appeared from behind the dark wood chest, his domed, hairless head unmistakable in the crystal light. But there was something about him that seemed different, not quite right. His posture, for one thing, was not as it had been before, when they had met him at the entrance to the cave. There he had been sort of bent and stooped, but now he was straight and erect with his chin up in the air. His clothing, while still the green velvet doublet, green leggings and pointed black boots, seemed now to be altogether smarter! His boots shone and his leggings were without wrinkles. The doublet had been brushed making the velvet nap glisten.

He was carrying before him a large tray, similar to the tea-tray on the other side of the bed. On it were two tall crystal wine glasses and three smaller glasses each filled to the brim with a dark claret liquid. A short, white towel was draped over his left arm. Grizel, indeed, seemed to be the perfect butler! "A drink of wine to celebrate your departure!" he announced in a clear voice that bore no relation to his earlier cackle.

"Thankyou, my loyal Master Grizel!" said Hester with a trusting smile. "You are right! We should toast our future and that of *Aqua Crysta*! Come, my friends, a drink before we leave the place that has been our home for the last three hundred years and more!"

With the aid of Grizelda, she hobbled forward and gestured to the others to join her in celebration. Jamie, still eying Grizel suspiciously despite his immaculate change of appearance, picked up one of the larger glasses for himself and one for his sister. Hester handed one of the smaller glasses to Grizelda and took one herself. Grizel took the last.

"What about us?" came a chorus of tiny voices from Jamie's T-shirt pocket.

Carefully, he removed the van and placed it on top of the chest. Lepho and the others jumped out onto the intricately carved and bejewelled lid.

"To our friends from *Aqua Crysta* and Jessica and Jamie!" exclaimed Hester.

"To the future!" called Grizel.

Glasses were raised in celebration and then the gathering took their first sips...with the exception of Grizel who gulped down his wine in one.

Suddenly, the tranquility of the lagoon was shattered!

"*All of you, STOP!!*" bellowed Lepho as loudly as he could. "*THROW YOUR GLASSES TO THE GROUND!!*"

At the same moment, as glasses rained around him, Grizel collapsed onto the crystal sand grasping his stomach and moaning in agony. About him, broken glasses spilled their deadly contents and the liquid burnt, spitted and smoked as it splattered the sugary sand!

Panic stricken, the rest spat their sips to the ground and fell on their knees in the shallows of the lake to wash their mouths.

Grizel writhed in agony as the life in him ebbed away.

His devoted sister cradled his head as he gasped his last words, "Beware...the *Lights*!...It was...the...only answer!...We should...have...*all died!*"

Then his eyes closed, his head fell limp in his sister's arms.

He was dead.

Silence fell upon the scene for what seemed like an eternity as the others considered what had happened...and how close they had all been to death.

"But how did you know, Lepho?" Jamie eventually asked, with a shudder and a tremble in his voice.

The tiny Aqua Crystan was standing at the edge of the chest lid pointing at a bottle lying in the sand. A bottle similar to all the others on the shelves of the alchemist's cellar with an ancient faded paper label clinging to its side.

Letters, written in black ink with a scratchy pen could just be seen.

"Hymlic Wine!" said Lepho sadly. "Made from hemlock...a deadly, deadly poison!"

Tears flowed from Grizelda's eyes as she lay her evil brother on the sand and began to cover him with the soft crystals. Hester quietly helped as the others silently watched the burial. Soon just a heap of sand was all there was to show Grizel's final resting place.

The little mound faded from view amid the clutter of furniture as the small boat drifted across the lake. The gentle sound of lapping oars was all that could be heard, as Jessica and Jamie pulled the craft across the glassy water. Hester and Grizelda sat at the stern rapt with sorrow and shame mixed with thoughts of what the future held. In front of them stood the ever patient chestnut mare watching the distant shore shrink to nothing.

Between Jessica and Jamie lay the golden bundle that wrapped the sleeping Gwenda and next to her was the *Ford 'T'* with Lepho, Jonathan and Jane perched quietly on the front seat. It was a sad, solemn voyage.

On and on the boat glided, cutting a gentle swash through the smooth glass. The forest of stalactites above, and their rippled reflections in the lake, both seemed endless, as did the vastness of the water.

It was after at least an hour of gentle rowing that Jessica suggested to Jamie that they rest. The oars stopped and were raised. The boat drifted in the eerie emptiness. All around was the shimmering water with no sign of a shore to be seen. The silence was so solid it could almost be touched.

Jessica and Jamie both had the same thoughts going round and round in their minds as they rowed steadily across the water...and it was Jessica, this time, who felt she just had to ask about the *'Lights'*... the very same ones that Grizel had warned them of in his last, dying breaths.

She looked at the sad, wizened pair sitting hunched up together at the back of the boat, and finally plucked up the nerve.

As the little boat drifted aimlessly in small circles, Hester mesmerised her audience as she told her magical tale which began way, way back in the years following the Great Fire of London of 1666.

She told of how Merrick, the elder brother of herself and Gwenda, had looked after them when they had all found themselves with the nasty Master of Soulsyke after their long trek north from London.

With tears welling in her eyes, she told of how the Master had sold the two young girls as child servants to a dealer from York, telling their brother that they had drowned when high waves had plucked them from the rocks near Whitby while they were scavaging for whelks and cockles to eat.

"We managed to escape and made our way back to the Moors from York to find Merrick, but he too, had mysteriously vanished. We spied upon *Old Soulsyke* from a safe distance but saw no sign of our brother. It was much later when we discovered that he had found sanctuary in a magical place called *Aqua Crysta*!"

She paused and looked sadly at her dying sister wrapped in the golden bundle.

"But we must carry on with our journey across the lake," she said. "Are you rested?"

Jessica and Jamie nodded, gripped their oars, and once again the gentle lapping of the water whispered as they rhythmically dipped the blades into the shimmering molten glass. With Hester's hand on the tiller, the boat nosed away into the pinky distance, but still, there was no sign of the far shore.

Hester continued with her tale.

"I remember that it had been a very chilly Winter's day," she began, casting her memory back to when all three had been together.

"Merrick, Gwenda and myself had been out gathering sticks for the fire at *Old Soulsyke*. It was just a few months before the Master sold us. As we trudged over the fields dragging our twine-bundled branches, the darkness of night was already drawn across the sky. We rested by one of the new walls and gazed up at the stars. We knew the Master would be late home so there was no hurry, although I do remember how quickly the coldness gripped us because we'd stopped."

She paused, loosened her hand from the tiller and pulled her red gown snugly around her, as though she was reliving the chill of the Winter's night.

"The cold urged us on...and we set upon the winding track that lead to the farmhouse...but then, as we passed the pool just below *Old Soulsyke*...we saw reflected in its face...a sight...a sight I shall *never* forget...!"

She paused once more, and Jessica and Jamie looked at one another, hardly able to keep their minds on their rowing.

"What did you see?" whispered Jamie, bursting to know the secrets of Hester's memories.

"*Lights*...perfectly round lights...maybe nine or ten of them...chasing, dancing in a circle! We looked above the pool...and there they were...

spinning faster and faster...faster and faster...until they blurred into *one bright white ring*...hovering above the water like a magnificent, brilliant halo...then they slowed and each hung around the pool with broad beams meeting above its centre...then in a mysterious mist at the place the beams met...a shape began to form...the shape of a..."

She stopped suddenly and pointed into the distance behind the rowers. Jessica and Jamie turned, their hearts pounding with excitement.

"The far shore is near, my friends!" announced Hester. "We shall soon be there!"

"But what was in the mists?" gasped Jessica, pulling strongly on her oar, dying to hear what was coming next!

"It was the shape of a *man*...a tall, white bearded man, with a kind face, wearing a golden gown that stretched to the water. He seemed to float before us like a ghost from a world beyond this. Then, as we stared into his radiance, he produced a perfectly formed, pointed peak of dazzling blood red crystal...that sparkled and shimmered in his long, slender fingers as though it had a life of its own. As we watched, transfixed by what we saw, he began to speak in a voice of such majesty and warmth. His words have remained with me ever since, and later, gave meaning to not only *our* lives by the *Golden Waters* but to those who have sought refuge in the realm of *Aqua Crysta*...!!"

Once again, she paused, lost in her memories and knowing the words held the key to the very existence of the two magical underworld kingdoms. Never, in over three long centuries, had she uttered them to anyone. Only herself, Gwenda and Merrick knew what the vision had said.

If her sister died as well as Merrick, then she alone would be the keeper of the secret.

She looked at Jessica and Jamie, then at the Aqua Crystans, desperately torn as to whether to reveal the secret words or not!

At last, she spoke, and the words that flowed from her lips astonished her listeners. Even Lepho was taken aback by her revelations concerning the origins of *Aqua Crysta!*

According to Hester, and there seemed no reason to doubt her, the blood red crystal, a *"Crystal of Eternity"* was one of many such crystals that had fallen to Earth from the stars. The land over which they had flown before striking the ground became transformed by powerful, magical forces and assumed strange qualities beyond human understanding.

Qualities brought from the unknown *Mother Star of the Crystals,* and qualities which were powerful enough to penetrate deep into the rocks of Planet Earth in the vicinity of where the crystals landed...but diminishing in power just a few miles away.

This shower of eternal crystals had struck the Earth thousands and thousands of years ago and throughout Man's history only three such crystals had been found. One near the ancient stone-circle of Stonehenge on the  Salisbury Plain, one near King Arthur's castle at Tintagel on the Cornish

 coast and one on the Yorkshire Moors near Whitby Abbey.

The finder of all three crystals was King Arthur's magician, a man blessed with immortality and known by Arthur as the *Guardian of the Crystals of Eternity.* His never ending task was to renew the powers of the crystals when they began to fade every three or four hundred years by lifting them from their landing places and casting a magical spell upon them!

"And that's what you saw him doing on that cold Winter's night!" said Jessica at last, revelling in the magic and her love of history.

"Yes, my friend," said Hester, "but it was his parting words that meant the most.

For as the lights around the pool began to spin and once again become a brilliant halo around him, he said...and these were his *exact* words...

'If I fail to return before you three die as one,
Then the Crystal's power will at last have gone'

"But how did you know that Merrick was going to die when you sent your first message to Aqua Crysta?" asked a puzzled Lepho. "And who told you that Gwenda and yourself would die within hours of your brother passing away?"

"How I knew that Merrick was going to die, I cannot tell. It came to me mysteriously one day while I was playing the harpsichord. I just had what you might call a premonition...a voice in the music...and then, of course, I remembered the words of the Guardian...'*you three die as one*'....so I *had* to *somehow* try and save Gwenda and myself by reaching the realm which lay nearer the powers of the *Crystal of Eternity*...the magic here was fading fast although it had never been as strong as in *Aqua Crysta*..."

"So that is why you are not as small as Lepho, and Jonathan and Jane," said Jamie. "The waters here are not quite as powerful."

"They have been quite powerful enough for our liking," sighed Hester, "but if we can reach *Aqua Crysta* we may live just a little longer until King Arthur's magician returns to hopefully renew the powers of the crystal. If only he could have returned to save our brother."

"But if he knows the crystal's power needs renewing, then why hasn't he appeared as he has done every three or four centuries for thousands of years?" asked Jessica, not quite understanding.

"I fear that something could have befallen him and the magic is over," sighed Hester once more. "He may *never* return and the crystal's power will die along with the rest of us! There is no certainty! All we can try and do is to prevent Gwenda and myself from dying...and our best chances of that lie in us reaching *Aqua Crysta*...the realm with the stronger magic of eternity!"

By now the far shore was closing fast and the same sugary sands could be seen, this time with no signs of antique furniture and the like. Soon the little boat glided up onto the beach and its passengers disembarked. From here, the shore from which they had rowed across the *Golden Lagoon* was invisible.

It had been a long journey but at least it had been smooth and trouble free for Gwenda who seemed comfortable in her golden bundle in Jessica's arms.

Hester and Grizelda led the way along the sands and it wasn't long before they reached an arched wooden door similar to the others they'd come across. Jamie overtook them and pushed it open. It swung open with a familiar, spine chilling creak and everyone jostled through, first casting a last glance at the splendours of the cavern.

Beyond the door it was dark and eyes had to adjust to the gloom, but when they had done so, they all caught sight of...

...a strange silhouette...in the shadows...

...lurking menacingly just above them...

...a strange silhouette with two enormous bright golden saucer shapes buried near the top...one moment there, the next moment gone...

...one moment there, the next moment gone!

Chapter 14

It was the unmistakable shape of the huge owl that Jessica and Jamie had last seen the night before, flying off into the dark sky from *Deer Leap*, with Lepho clasped beneath in the basket.

"Ah, our loyal messenger, Merlyn, the owl named by Lucius, our own sadly missed chief alchemist and magician!" announced Hester with a mixture of pride and regret.

The owl swivelled its head from side to side and continued blinking its fiery eyes. Other than light from the cavern creeping under the door, its eyes were the only illumination in the darkness, but they shone brightly enough to light up the faces of its sudden company. It didn't seem concerned at all by the arrival of the travellers. In fact, it almost appeared to have been expecting them!

"What happened to Lucius?" asked Jamie. "We met him in that spooky room up the spiral staircase!"

"Jamie! For goodness sake show a bit of respect!" snapped Jessica, nudging him sharply with her elbow. "We didn't exactly meet him. It was just a skeleton!"

"Don't worry, my friend. I know what your brother means!" smiled Hester.

"Lucius, himself, would laugh if he were with us today. He was a wonderful man and the most powerful and wise magician of his time. It was a sad day for us all when he took his own life in much the same way that Grizel did!"

"He killed himself?...in his room?" gasped Jamie.

"He did indeed, much to our regret!" sighed Hester.

"But why?" asked Jessica.

"It happened nearly two centuries ago," said Hester, gazing into the eyes of the owl. "Just after the twenty or so people who lived here by the *Golden Lagoon* had decided to cut ourselves off from the Outside World and stop dispensing *Golden Water* to the never ending visitors from all over England. Lucius had just joined us a few months before and taken up residence in the ancient cellar beneath the *Needle Crag*...along with Merlyn, his owl..."

"You mean that Merlyn is *two hundred years old*?" burst Jessica, looking with astonishment at the owl, but almost immediately realising that nothing she heard should ever surprise her!

"Even older perhaps!" said Hester. "For his two birds were well tamed and loyal to Lucius even on the day he arrived."

"Two birds?" queried Jessica. "There was a *pair* of owls?"

"No, just the one owl perched gloriously on his shoulder, and the other was in a gilded cage. I remember him standing at the mouth of the outer cave and introducing himself and asking us to take him in.

Of course, he was well known and famed throughout England for his magic and sorcery.

We were delighted to have him and he was equally delighted with his room. Before long it was packed from floor to ceiling with his bottles of potions which he'd brought with him by horse and cart from the south of England. He even fell in love with Grizelda and gave her his horse, *Gabrielle*...the one you see here, still unseparable from my loyal friend and servant after all these years!"

Jessica and Jamie, once more amazed by what they were hearing, looked at Grizelda, standing quietly by her mistress, holding the reins of the chestnut mare.

"Lucius even conjured up a potion from his magic powders mixed with the *Golden Waters* to shrink Gabrielle, so Grizelda could ride her. It worked with the horse but he was unsuccessful in shrinking himself and his faithful birds. They, and Lucius always remained a size to match the Outside World."

"What kind of bird was in the gilded cage?" asked Jessica.

"Oh, she was a wonderful bird...a singer of exquisite songs...he called her '*Nemue*'...she was a beautiful and enchanting *nightingale!*"

"A *nightingale!!*" chorused Jessica and Jamie, spellbound by Hester's words.

"You mean the nightingale we heard in the forest yesterday...the one that guided us with *Chandar*, the albino deer, to the pool?" Jamie gasped.

Hester nodded and smiled in the golden glow from Merlyn's eyes.

"Yes, my friends, and, as you can see, the powerful magic of Lucius is still with us long after his death! It is alive by some miraculous means in the souls of *Merlyn*, his owl and *Nemue*, his nightingale...and even in *Chandar*, the young deer!"

"But why did he take his own life?" repeated Jessica.

"Alas, that has always remained a mystery!" admitted Hester. "Although he did talk of some terrible disaster that had befallen him before he came to us...but he never could bring himself to tell us of its nature. Whatever it was, he spent day after day in his room trying to conjure spells, magic and potions to undo the tragedy he had encountered. He worked feverishly as though possessed by some deep, burdensome guilt...until he could go on no longer...and that was when, rapt with failure, he took his own life!"

Hester paused and, in the dark silence, the sound of sorrowful sobbing softly echoed. It was Grizelda, overwhelmed by grief. Not only had she just buried her brother and endured his shameful deeds...but now her memories of the death of her beloved Lucius had cast her deeper into depths of painful despair. Her heart was truly broken.

Hester put a loving arm around her shoulders and whispered words in her ear.

Grizelda dried her eyes and began to loosen the tiny buttons of her green gown just below her chin. Her small, frail fingers undid one, two, three buttons and then she brought slowly into the open, a large, circular disc of decorated gold. It looked like a huge medallion glinting in the light from Merlyn's eyes.

On it was a carved ring of overlapping oak leaves surrounding a crown with a single dagger lain across it. The medallion was held in place by a delicate chain around Grizelda's neck.

"Take comfort from Lucius's charm," said Hester. "You know it always warms your heart and spirit."

Grizelda stroked the amulet which seemed to hang so heavily...and soon a loving smile beamed across her wrinkled face.

"Lucius gave it to her on the day he died," explained Hester. "She's worn it ever since, tucked away beneath her..."

Hester's words were suddenly drowned by the most tremendous shriek from Merlyn that completely filled the darkness! Everyone gazed at the owl's silhouette as its great wings spread to their fullest extent!

As the shriek's echoes faded, another shriek pierced the air almost forcing the watchers to cover their ears!

The owl's eyes seemed to grow bigger and brighter as it stared intently at the glinting medallion that Grizelda had exposed!

Then, the most miraculous, awe-inspiring happening occurred that left the travellers at once bewildered and open mouthed with wonder!

Merlyn plunged into the air, swept above their heads with beating wings and for a moment vanished from view in the dark.

But an instant later, candle wicks burst into flame all around them as though they'd been switched on!

Dozens of them, all at once flooding the darkness with light!

And then before them, a wide stone staircase appeared, delving steeply downwards into a rocky passage, edged with dozens of more candle flames! They could see the great owl swooping gracefully above the scores of steps, and as it shrank into the deep distance, more and more candles lit the splendid stairway!

"What's happening? What's happening?" came muffled voices from Jamie's T-shirt pocket. Jamie grasped the little van and let the equally amazed Aqua Crystans look at the wondrous sight that had simply appeared from nowhere!

"It's the ancient staircase that leads to a secret, hidden entrance in the valley below!" explained Hester. "But to see it illuminated in such a way is beyond my understanding!"

"It was as though Grizelda's medallion sparked some kind of spell on Merlyn!" said Jessica, her face lit brightly by the flickering candles.

"There is one thing that is certain," said Lepho calmly from the front seat of the *Ford 'T'*. "We have to follow the owl...and with all the haste we can muster!!"

Without another word, Jamie gathered Hester and Grizelda up in his arms and headed down the staircase.

Jessica followed, still cradling the sleeping Gwenda, and behind trotted the chestnut mare, *Gabrielle*, like a dog at heel.

With the sounds of pattering feet and clattering hoofs ringing around them, Jessica and Jamie darted down the steps as quickly as they could.

On and on, the staircase delved into the rocky depths, constantly lit by the two rows of candle flames which flickered and danced as they passed.

"All I can say..." panted Jamie, "is that I'm glad we're not *climbing* this lot!"

As he glanced behind at his sister, hardly
daring to take his eyes off the
never ending steps, he saw darkness
swiftly in pursuit.
"The candles are going out as soon as
we've passed them!" he gasped.
"It's incredible!"
"Watch where you're going, Jamie!"
warned Jessica. "This must be the longest

staircase ever! Remember its length must be the same as our climb this
morning! If you trip now you'll be rolling for ever!"

Fortunately this time, Jamie didn't manage to fall
head over heels with his precious passengers, and, after what seemed
like hundreds of steps, he could just make out the end of the staircase
at last!
"I can see daylight ahead!" he shouted. "We're nearly there!"

As the last candle flames magically vanished into
plumes of wispy smoke, Jessica and Jamie jumped off the very last step
into a damp, mossy corridor cut into the rock. Ahead was the entrance
Hester had mentioned...a bright, sunlit circle of green accompanied by
the sound of trickling water.

Hester and Grizelda squinted in the brilliance as
Jamie walked along the short, rock-cut passage. Moments later, he and
his sister were standing by the stream...the one which wound its way
along the floor of Newtondale Gorge!
They were back in the *Outside World*!...and the sun was still shining
brightly in a brilliant blue sky!

But...it was at that very moment that they noticed
it...or rather *felt* it...!
Something peculiar was happening *beneath their feet*!
"It's *shaking*, the ground's *shaking*!" Jessica exclaimed, staring at the
pebbly shore.
"And what's *that*? Listen!" shouted Hester from Jamie's arms, suddenly

alarmed by her first visit to the Outside World for years.

A deep, grinding rumble was thundering towards them...louder and louder!

The ground shook more and more!

"*What is it? Please tell me!*" came another voice that shocked everyone as much as the thunderous din and the ground shaking!

It was Grizelda!

"But she hasn't uttered a *single word* since the day Lucius died!" exclaimed Hester, unable to believe her own ears. "Since the very same day he gave her that charm around her...! Grizelda, *where is it?* It's *gone!*"

Then, just as Grizelda looked down, panic-stricken to see that her gold medallion had, indeed, been lost, the source of the ground shaking, thunderous rumble appeared!!

"It's the train back to Goathland!" bellowed Jamie above the noise.

In a trice, the monstrous black, iron railway engine was upon them, towering above the fence on the other side of the stream, its pumping pistons belching out clouds of hissing, spitting, steamy vapour!

From below it seemed vast and fearsome like a monster from the fiery depths of the Earth...especially to Hester and Grizelda who had never been so close to one of the 'iron horses' which chugged up and down the valley every day!

Then came the clicketty-click, clicketty-click of the countless, spinning, iron wheels of the carriages. Clicketty-click!...clicketty-click!

Next, a deafening, hollow whistle suddenly struck through the thunder of the clattering din of rolling iron wheels upon the iron rails and the constant hissing of the steam!

The petrified chestnut mare could stand it no longer!

With a wild, snorting whinny and a lashing swish of her head and tail, she galloped and splashed into the shallows of the stream.

"After her!" shouted Jamie, still holding the bewildered and confused Hester and Grizelda. "She's following the train!"

"The engine's slowing down!" gasped Jessica, following behind.
"It must be coming into the platform at Newtondale Station!"
As the two of them splashed through the shallows, they could see the long wooden platform stretching before them, with groups of hikers dotted along it waiting to catch the train to Goathland.
"We've got to catch it!" yelled Jamie. "It's the fastest way back to *Aqua Crysta*!"

The engine and five carriages gradually came to a standstill and doors began to swing open. Passengers stepped off onto the platform and the waiting ones boarded.
Jamie and Jessica splashed into deeper water and crossed the stream. *Gabrielle* was struggling in the depths but Jessica managed to haul the horse out of the water with her free arm while trying her best to cradle Gwenda.
They bounded up the bank and onto the platform, just as another deafening whistle split the air!
Then the engine at the far end of the platform bellowed a great cloud of smoke into the air!
"It's going to set off!!" panted Jamie breathlessly.
"We're going to miss it!!"

Chapter 15

Just as the engine was about to pull away from the platform, the nearest door of the last carriage sprung open and a familiar figure leaned out.

"Hurry!" he cried. "You'll just make it!"

When the white-haired old man wearing the grey waistcoat and spotted bow-tie saw who he was encouraging to catch his train, he began to wish he hadn't!

It was the ticket-inspector!!

Not only had the poor man not yet recovered from the shocks he'd endured on the 7:30 train from Goathland that same morning, but now he was faced with a pair of dripping children, a dripping dog (*'it is a dog, isn't it?'* he thought to himself) and a load of old dolls!

As the carriages jolted and shuddered into motion, Jessica and Jamie scrambled aboard.

"You cooled down in the stream, did you?" asked the old man, looking disapprovingly at the pairs of soggy jeans and trainers and the trail of water along the corridor. "Well make sure you don't sit on my clean seats! You can stand to Goathland! It's not far! And keep that peculiar dog off 'em as well!"

Jessica and Jamie hurried into the first empty compartment and slid the door closed behind them.

"Better do as he says," said Jessica, "or he'll only come barging in again!"

She carefully placed Gwenda on one of the two long floral patterned seats and Jamie sat Hester and Grizelda next to the golden bundle. *Gabrielle*, having somewhat calmed down, stood on the floor between the seats still dripping.

"I'm amazed that Gwenda's still asleep after all that!" said Jamie, looking at the peaceful face of Hester's sister.

"She has been in a deep sleep for days now," whispered Hester.

"She surely cannot have long to live in this World!"

Grizelda again began to sob and Hester comforted her.

"We'll find your precious charm that Lucius gave to you," she whispered, "but for the moment be happy of heart that your voice has returned!"

"I would rather have my charm than my voice," replied Grizelda sadly. "Now I have nothing! Lucius begged me to keep it for as long as I lived, along with his deepest, darkest secret!"

"What secret?" asked Jessica, rocking from side to side as the train picked up speed.

"I still cannot say even though I now have a voice," said Grizelda. "I often think that wearing the charm made me lose my speech and eased the burden of keeping the secret!"

"That would make some kind of sense," said Hester, "as you lost your voice the day Lucius died! The day he gave you the medallion!"

"Perhaps Lucius put a spell on the charm that made sure you would never tell his secret!" burst Jamie, beginning to feel like a detective.

Grizelda looked at him with sorrowful eyes and nodded.

"You are correct," she said, "but please, please, do not ask me to say any more. I beg you."

Jessica, realising that Grizelda was becoming even more upset and confused, quickly changed the subject and gave her brother one of her warning nudges with her elbow.

"We'll soon be in Goathland!" she cheerfully announced. "Then we can ring dad!"

Hester looked puzzled.

"'*Ring dad?*'" she asked. "What is the meaning of your words?"

"Sorry about that!" laughed Jessica. "I mean we'll telephone our father!"

"I still do not understand," insisted Hester. "What is this '*telephone*' of which you speak?"

"It's a gadget for talking to people who are miles away!" smiled Jessica.

"A '*gadget*'? What's a '*gadget*'?" asked Hester. "You talk in riddles! With words I do not under..."

Suddenly Hester froze as if she'd seen a ghost, her eyes fixed on something behind Jessica and Jamie.

Jessica turned just in time to see the old ticket-inspector sliding open the compartment door.

"Glad to see you're not sitting on the seats!" he smiled, staring curiously at the dolls. "Can I see your tickets, please?"

Jessica delved into her back pocket, but just at that moment disaster struck!

The carriage suddenly jolted and Grizelda, who was trying her best to keep absolutely still, felt herself slipping from the edge of the seat.

She shot out her arms to steady herself, but it was too late! In a flurry of waving arms and legs she plummeted to the floor and collapsed in a heap of green velvet.

The ticket-inspector couldn't believe his eyes!

One of the dolls with the wizened old faces had come to life!

He stood there, rooted to the spot, his mouth wide open and his eyes almost popping out of their sockets!

Then...to make things even worse...*Gabrielle* suddenly reared up on her hind legs, whinnied in alarm and galloped over the black, polished boots of the old man, through the open door and into the corridor!

Grizelda staggered to her feet and stumbled after her beloved chestnut mare, calling her name as loudly as she could.

The ticket-inspector looked upon the happenings around his feet with stunned disbelief...and then he himself collapsed onto one of the seats next to Hester, loosened his collar and rubbed his eyes.

"Th..that was a h..horse and an old l..lady!" he mumbled, as Jessica dashed into the corridor in pursuit of Grizelda.

"We'll pay the extra fare!" she called, as she disappeared and pushed her way past other astonished passengers standing in the corridor watching the strange, miniature horse and lady pelting along the narrow passageway!

"Stop this monstrous machine!!" demanded Hester, suddenly springing to life and rapping the dazed ticket-inspector on the knee with her tiny fists. "Stop it at once!"

The old man gave one last gasp of amazement, his eyes rolled, his head fell backwards and then...he fainted!

Hester scrambled to the floor and, she too, with a sudden burst of youthful energy sped off into the corridor!

Jamie quickly picked up Gwenda and Jessica's rucksack, rushed out of the compartment and darted after her between the bewildered, speechless passengers.

Fortunately for all concerned, the train was beginning to slow down as it came into Goathland Station. Hikers and holiday makers began to flock towards the carriage doors and Grizelda managed to catch up with *Gabrielle* in the forest of passengers' legs. The late afternoon train was so crowded that no one noticed as she grabbed the reins and pulled herself up onto the saddle. Just behind, in the hustle and bustle, Hester wove her way through the maze of hiking boots, sandals and baby buggies...and, as the train came to a halt, she caught up with Grizelda who pulled her up onto the chestnut mare's back.

Then, just as a nosy poodle was showing just a little too much interest in the peculiar canine with riders on its back, all the carriage doors flew open and torrents of passengers poured from the train onto the platform. Jessica and Jamie emerged from one door just as *Gabrielle* sprang from another, throwing the thronging mass of waiting passengers and alighting ones into a sudden state of frozen confusion!

Every single pair of eyes was transfixed by the sight of the diminutive horse with its riders galloping along the platform, past a collection of milk churns and through a large doorway which lead out of the station. Every spectator just stopped and stared, dumb-struck by what they'd seen...all that is, except for Jessica and Jamie, who ran between the dozens of spellbound statues, hoping to catch up with *Gabrielle* just beyond the station entrance.

But...they were too late!

As they rushed past the ticket office and through the main doorway, they looked around in desperation for their new found friends from the *Golden Waters*...but they'd vanished!

Vanished into thin air!

Would they *ever* see them again?

"So Jim Murphy managed to fix the back light?" Jessica asked her father as the Land Rover trundled along the narrow moorland lane back to *Deer Leap*, and she tried to steady her rucksack on her knee which now held the secretly sleeping Gwenda!

She tried to sound interested but her thoughts, as well as Jamie's, were miles away. They both knew that they had let Hester and Grizelda down. They just hoped that somehow the two of them would find the pool near *Old Soulsyke*, although they knew it would be a rough and dangerous overland journey especially on a horse no larger than a cocker spaniel! The three or four miles would seem like a hundred!

"Yes, and he fixed the problem with the engine!" replied Mr Dawson. "He's just got a bit of body-work to do on the rear bumper, but there's no rush for that! Have you two had a good day exploring Pickering?"

"Not bad," mumbled Jamie sadly.

"Well you could have fooled me!" laughed his father. "To say it's your birthday, son, you sound really down in the dumps! What's up with the pair of you?"

Mr Dawson clamped his hand on Jamie's knee and then withdrew it quickly.

"Why on earth are your jeans damp on a day like this?" he smiled.

"He went for a paddle in the river and fell in as usual!" chipped in Jessica, thinking quickly.

Then she changed the subject.

"Dad," she asked dreamily, "do you know anything about *Stonehenge* or *King Arthur*?"

Mr Dawson slowed down to allow a sheep and a couple of lambs to cross the road and then the Land Rover gently picked up speed again.

"Well, all I know about Stonehenge is that it's a circle of huge standing stones put up by the ancient Druids thousands of years ago. It's in Wiltshire, somewhere near Salisbury. I think the ancient folk used it as a kind of clock, telling the time of the year by shadows cast by the stones. To be honest, I don't know much about it, I'm afraid!"

"What about *King Arthur*?" asked Jessica.

"Ah, now that's a different kettle of fish!" beamed her father. "I've got loads of books about King Arthur! Ask me anything you want to know about his wife, *Guinevere*, or *Camelot Castle*, or his '*Knights of the Round Table*', or his sword, '*Excalibur*', or *Sir Lancelot*, or the *Search for the Holy Grail*, or *Merlyn...*"

"Merlyn!!" exclaimed Jessica and Jamie, nearly causing their dad to jump out of his skin.

"Merlyn? Who was Merlyn, dad?" burst Jessica.

Mr Dawson turned off the moorland road and the Land Rover bumped and bounced along the grassy track towards *Deer Leap*.

"Merlyn," said Mr Dawson slowly, welcoming his children's enthusiasm for one of his heroes, "was the power behind the throne! King Arthur's right-hand man! He was the King's trusty friend and advisor. But, he was even more than that!"

The Land Rover came to a halt in front of the stone cottage and Mr Dawson switched off the engine.

His voice dropped to a whisper as Jessica and Jamie gazed at him, wondering what was coming next!

"Merlyn, kids, was the most wonderful magician and wizard who ever lived!!!"

Jessica and Jamie looked at one another speechless...but what their father said next set their heartbeats racing with excitement!

"Along with, of course, his lover, the magical 'Lady of the Lake', his beloved *Nemue*!!"

With the sounds of '*Merlyn*' and '*Nemue*', the names of the owl and nightingale, ringing in their ears, Jessica and Jamie rushed into the cottage, firing one question after another at their bewildered father to answer.

Mr Dawson lead them into his study and reached for several large books from the top shelf of his bookcase.

"Here, have a look at these!" he enthusiastically suggested. "These will answer all your questions. Take them upstairs, while I sort out the plan of action for tonight with the police!"

With their arms full of books, Jessica and Jamie stopped in their tracks.

"What do you mean, '*plan of action*'?" asked Jamie.

"The deer poachers!" said their father. "The police have had a tip off that the gang are meeting at the pool near *Old Soulsyke* tonight just after sunset. So we're going to be waiting for 'em!"

"But, dad, they'll have guns!" burst Jessica, with all sorts of thoughts rushing through her mind about dangers for her dad, as well as for poor Hester and Grizelda!

"Don't worry about me, Jess!" reassured her father. "The police will outnumber them easily, so they'll give 'emselves up without a fight!

Believe me, those ruffians are no more than cowards, skulking around in the dark, killing defenceless animals!"

"Can we come then?" ventured Jamie, knowing perfectly well what the answer would be!

"No, son. I think it'd be best for you two to stay here tonight, out of the way! I'll tell you all about what happens when I get back!"

Mr Dawson looked grimly at his children.

"Promise you won't go out into the forest tonight!" he said sternly, his blue eyes piercing theirs.

"We promise!" chorused Jessica and Jamie, although thoughts about the magical quest they had fallen into were beginning to flash uncontrollably through their minds as they spoke.

After all, other promises had already been made...and the magic...although they didn't know it...was still with them!!

They could sense that things of great significance and magnitude were about to happen that night in the forest they called *George*...and they both knew perfectly well that they just *had* to be there..

...whatever the danger!!

Chapter 16

It was exactly two hours later when Jamie blew as hard as he could and watched the ten candle flames flutter and vanish. "I hope you've remembered to make a wish!" said his father with a smile.

As the ten wisps of blue smoke faded above his birthday cake, Jamie couldn't help thinking of the candle flames which had illuminated the steep stone staircase from the *Golden Lagoon*. Next to the cake on the kitchen table was the Eagle Owl feather from the morning.

He picked it up and thought of Merlyn silently swooping and skimming above the stone steps.

"I think that feather needs to kept somewhere special!" said Jessica.

Jamie quickly removed one of his candles from his cake and replaced it with the beautiful, mottled browny gold quill.

"There, that'll do until you think of somewhere!" he laughed.

He looked at his sister and together they made the same silent wish that everything would work out fine at the pool near *Old Soulsyke*.

"Well, I hope you've had a good birthday, son!" said Mr Dawson, leaving the kitchen table. "But I'm going to have to miss out on a slice of cake until I get back! I said I'd meet Sergeant Phillips and his men at about eight o'clock so I'd better make tracks!"

"It's been a great birthday, dad!" beamed Jamie. "Especially the train ride and the *Clan Campbell*!"

He carefully lifted the model from the table.

"I think I'll take it upstairs and put it on my book shelf," he said, inspecting the wonderful detail of the wheels and steam pistons.

Once again his mind raced back to the middle of the afternoon when a real steam engine had roared past them all as they'd stood by the stream near Newtondale Station.

"It looks as though we're in for another thunder storm tonight!" said Mr Dawson, as he put on his waterproof and slipped into his wellies.

Indeed, the setting sun had already been blotted out by dark clouds gathering in the west, and Jessica and Jamie wondered whether the forest was in for the same firework-show it had seen the night before!

"Right then, I'll see you two later!" said Mr Dawson, as he opened the kitchen door and stepped into the porch. Then, with one last glance back, he warned,

"And make sure you two keep your promise! OK?"

"OK!" called Jessica and Jamie, "and good luck!!"

Their father smiled, gave them a quick thumbs-up sign, and was gone.

"I do hope he'll be alright out there!" sighed Jessica as she cut a couple of slices of cake.

"Of course he will!" reassured her brother. "He'll be back safe and sound in no time! C'mon, let's take Jonathan, Jane and Lepho some cake. They deserve it after the journey they've had this afternoon!"

With Jamie holding his steam engine leading the way, the two of them climbed the cottage stairs. But just as Jamie creaked the third step from the top, they both suddenly stopped!

They could hear something coming from Jessica's bedroom...a sort of sorrowful, wailing sound!

"Where am I?" moaned the voice. "Where am I?"

"It's too loud to be one of the Aqua Crystans!" whispered Jamie, creeping on tiptoes towards the bedroom door.

Jessica crept by him and slowly turned the handle.

"Then that means it must be...!" she whispered as she gently pushed open the door.

And, it was!

For there, sitting on the edge of the bed in a sort of white, lacy nightgown, was Gwenda!

She had, at long, long last, come out of her deep sleep...and was sitting there looking much livelier and healthier than the last time they'd seen her!

She even had roses in her cheeks!

Jessica and Jamie slowly tiptoed into the room so as not to alarm their guest. After all, Gwenda hadn't yet met them. The shock of seeing their size for the first time might have terrible results!

But, they needn't have worried, for as soon as Gwenda spotted her hosts, she just smiled and complained, "The last thing I heard was my sister playing the harpsichord, but now I find myself sitting on the edge of a strange bed in a strange room. Where am I? Where is my beautiful bed? Where is Hester? But before you answer, I must tell you that I feel so much better!"

She smiled again and ran her fingers through her long, grey, wispy hair.

She looked very much like her twin sister, but she seemed younger. Indeed, she looked even more like a doll than Hester because of her delicate, white nightdress and her miniature stockinged feet protruding from its hem.

Jessica thought that she'd better introduce herself.

"I am Jessica and this is my brother, Jamie," she said quietly, as she sat next to the small, almost porcelain-like figure.

"She's only just woken up!" squeaked Jane's voice from the top drawer next to the bed.

"And so have we actually!" yawned Jonathan. "That journey, Jamie, in your shirt pocket from the bottom of the stone staircase, and through the stream was absolutely awful! We were thrown about all over the place in the van! I'm just glad that we had that soft bedding inside to cushion our falls!"

"I'm very sorry about that," admitted Jamie, "but there was nothing else I could do! Apologies once more! Have some birthday cake to help make up for it!"

Just then, Lepho crawled out of the spiralled whelk shell.

"Did someone mention food?" he yawned while stretching his arms. "Let us eat while we discuss the next part of our Quest!"

While their guests nibbled the slices of birthday cake, Jessica and Jamie pored over the books from their father's study and told Gwenda what had happened while she had been in her deep sleep.

It was decided that *somehow*, despite the promise to Mr Dawson, they *all* had to reach the pool near *Old Soulsyke*!

Soon, all the books were scattered over Jessica's duvet. Jamie had the three Aqua Crystans sitting on the palm of his left hand while he turned pages with the other. Gwenda seemed quite happy leafing through a large book, looking for anything to do with Merlyn and Nemue.

There was plenty on the exploits of the noble knights, Bedivere, Galahad, Gawain, Tristan, Lancelot and the rest of the 'Knights of the Round Table', but not much on the two magicians. Camelot, King Arthur's castle was described in detail, as too was his magic sword, *'Excalibur'*.

"It seems that Nemue appeared one day walking over the waters of a lake in the Great Forest," said Jessica, her eyes glued to a page in one of the books.

"King Arthur and Merlyn were watching from the shore as she skimmed gracefully through the mists towards them. Then a hand rose out of the water grasping a sword. Nemue plucked the sword from the hand and gave it to the young King, saying that its name was 'Excalibur' and that it was forged by the blacksmiths of a wonderful, magical kingdom called 'Avalon'!!"

"That's the name Merrick gave to the island where we laid him after he died!" exclaimed Lepho. "He was always talking about the day he would eventually visit the timeless *Kingdom of Avalon!*"

"Hang on, there's more about Nemue here!" said Jessica. "Apparently, Merlyn, Arthur's magician, loved Nemue...but she didn't think much about him! It says here that she was a brilliant singer and could turn herself into a...*nightingale*...whenever she wanted!!"

"And I've read in this book," gasped Jamie, "that Merlyn, famed for his wisdom, could change himself into *an owl*!! And that ever since, people have thought of owls as being wise!"

Jamie closed his book and slowly stood up. He rubbed his chin thoughtfully and looked at Lepho who was standing on his palm. "Lepho, it *can't* be true...*can it?*" he asked quietly. "The owl and the nightingale we saw yesterday...can't possibly be *Merlyn* and *Nemue* from the time of King Arthur?"

"All things are possible, my friend!" replied Lepho. "But what I cannot understand is why they have been in the guise of two birds for over *two hundred Upper World years*!! If they were such powerful magicians, why didn't they change back into their human form?"

"Perhaps their spell went wrong somehow!" squeaked Jane.

"Or perhaps," said Gwenda, solemnly, "our good friend, Lucius, overpowered their magic when they met!"

"Lucius met Merlyn and Nemue?" gasped Jessica. "But that's impossible! Surely Lucius lived centuries after Merlyn and Nemue!"

"Of that we cannot be sure!" said Lepho. "Remember what I said about the impossible being possible! Is it not possible that these magicians and wizards have lived for thousands of years?"

"And, as I am sure my sister told you," said Gwenda, "when Lucius arrived at the *Golden Waters*, he carried with him an owl he called 'Merlyn' and a nightingale he called 'Nemue'!"

"So you think that in some kind of wizard's contest they became sort of stuck as an owl and a nightingale...!" gasped Jamie.

"...And Lucius blamed himself, and tried to come up with another spell of his own to change them back...!" said Jonathan.

"...And he couldn't, however much he tried, and that's why he took his own life in his room!" exclaimed Jessica.

It was then, at that very moment, that Gwenda suddenly got to her feet and pointed at the book that was lying before her on the duvet!

She had a look of such amazement on her face as she stared at the pages, it was as though she'd seen a ghost!

"That's it!" her voice echoed round the bedroom. "Merlyn is the *Guardian of the Crystals of Eternity*! He is the one that found them, and he is the one who has to renew their powers...but he cannot, because he is an owl!!! The proof is here...in front of your eyes!!"

Everyone gazed at the black ink drawings on the two pages. On the left was a beautiful sketch of Grizelda's lost medallion, with all the details of the ring of overlapping oakleaves, the crown and the dagger...and on the right was the reverse of the medallion...the side that Grizelda had never allowed anyone to see...and engraved on it in Old English letters were the words...

"Guardian of the Crystals of Eternity"

"But what are those other letters?" wondered Jamie,

135

pointing to a ring of strange symbols encircling the Old English inscription.

No one could make head nor tail of the mystical language, but as they all gazed at the magic circle there came such an explosion of sound from the other side of the room that they all nearly jumped out of their skins!

From nowhere, Merlyn the Owl had suddenly landed on the window-sill and was striking his enormous wings wildly on the panes - indeed, so frantically was he beating his wings that it seemed he would shatter the glass at any second!

"What's that hanging from his beak?" exclaimed Lepho.

"It's Grizelda's medallion!" burst Jessica. "The same one that's in the book!"

"And look!" cried Jane. "The circle of strange letters are glowing as brightly as the owl's eyes!"

Jessica rushed from her bed over to the window to get a closer look at the fiery, golden ring. In her arms was the book...and amazingly, as the dazzling ring of letters grew brighter on the medallion, so too, did the same mystical symbols on the ink sketched illustration!

"The book's tingling in my hands like nettle stings!" she shouted from the window. "It's the *magic*! It's the same magic I felt yesterday afternoon! I can't believe it!"

Then, before her eyes, the letters in the book began to dance. They began to change shape within the golden radiance. They began to change into words she could recognise!

"I can read the circle!" she exclaimed excitedly. "I can read what the message says!"

By now, Gwenda had slipped off the bed and had rushed over to Jessica, along with Jamie carrying the Aqua Crystans. They all stared at the magic that had taken place on the page of the book. Jessica looked at Merlyn through the glass and, as though she was part of the wondrous and miraculous spell, she began to speak the mysterious words that were written in the magical circle!

Chapter 17

"NO MORE TOMORROWS, FROM NOW I SAY, FOREVER CRYSTAL, FOREVER TODAY"

And then, at the very same moment as Jessica read the last word, the whole window was transformed into a spectacular, blinding square of brilliant gold!

The onlookers shielded their eyes from the glare...but just seconds later, when they dared to peep through their fingers...the brilliance had vanished...and with it the owl!

"He's gone! Merlyn's gone!" exclaimed Gwenda. "*We have to follow him*! Those words you read were the ones that the *Guardian of the Crystals* said on that cold Winter's night when I was returning to *Old Soulsyke* with Merrick and Hester all those years ago!"

"So, Merlyn the Owl, King Arthur's Merlyn and the *Guardian of the Crystals of Eternity* are all one and the same...!" burst Jane from Jamie's hand.

"And, somehow, he has been trapped in the guise of an owl since he met Lucius!" interrupted Lepho, "...*until now*!!"

"What do you mean, '*until now*?" asked Jessica.

Lepho paced up and down on Jamie's palm, rubbing his chin and occasionally scratching his head.

"I have come to the conclusion," he eventually began, "that Lucius somehow obtained the magic medallion from Merlyn before changing him into an owl and Nemue into a nightingale. Without the medallion they have been powerless to change back ever since...and when Merlyn the Owl saw the precious amulet hanging from Grizelda's neck at the top of the stone staircase, he grabbed it, but he still needed someone to read the magic spell in its glittering, gold letters!"

"And that was *you*, sis!" said Jamie, looking at Jessica...but Jessica was miles away, staring at the letters on the drawing in the book.

"Look!" she whispered. "The words are changing back into those strange symbols again. I can feel the tingle of stinging nettles in my fingertips! Feel the page, Jamie!"

Jamie gently touched the page.

"I can't feel a thing!" he muttered, sadly disappointed. "The magic must only be with you!"

"Fear not, my friend!" exclaimed Lepho. "The magic is with us all!! And we must make haste to the pond near *Old Soulsyke* to see wonders that none of us will believe possible! But at least it will mean that the powers of the *Crystals of Eternity* will have been renewed and the realms of *Aqua Crysta* and the *Golden Waters* will be safe for centuries to come!!"

Jessica placed the book on her bed with the others, and wrapped Gwenda in her golden sheet, while Jamie ushered Lepho and Jonathan and Jane into the *Ford 'T'*.

Then, not even thinking of their promise to their father, they skipped along the landing and down the stairs, Gwenda like a doll in Jessica's arms and the three Aqua Crystans in the van in Jamie's shirt pocket.

All their minds were full of what was to come. Full to the brim...and even spilling over!

Jessica reached the front door and opened it...but what she saw before her, standing patiently on the grassy track, made her, once again, gasp in amazement!

For there was the young albino deer, *Chandar,* with Nemue the Nightingale perched on one of her velvet budding horns!

There was no question as to why she was there, and without a moment's hesitation Jessica and Jamie mounted her.
Nemue took to the air, leading the way, and *Chandar* followed.
As the sun slowly set, the nimble deer picked up speed and plunged into the depths of the forest.

They would be there in next to no time...
                    ...to witness the spectacle of a life-time!

As daylight dissolved into the blackness of the night, the warm, still air of the forest became heavier and heavier with clinging moisture. Above, the towering, dark clouds seemed to be gathering for the storm of all storms! If last night's performance had been a symphony, then tonight's would be an overture! An overture to end all overtures!
        The children tightly clung to *Chandar* and to one another as she sprinted gracefully through the ranks of spruce and larch, leaping over the never ending ridges of fallen needles.
Nemue flew ahead, occasionally alighting onto a branch and piercing the clammy air with a few, beautiful shrill notes of her familiar song. And, on and on, *Chandar* followed the musical beckonings of the magical signpost!
        The first flash of forked lightning split the dark sky like an angry, jagged line of chalk on a blackboard!
A second later it had vanished and its sister, a rumble of thunder grumbled her first mumblings of discontent!

        At the same moment, the concealed policemen near *Old Soulsyke's* pond watched eagerly as three unwary rogues...the deer poachers...made their way along the narrow path towards the small stretch of water. Each pulled his anorak hood over his head as the first drops of rain fell from the sky, and their leader pointed to the shelter of the ruined barn.

"We'd best take cover in there before we get soaked!" came the rough voice of the leader, brandishing his shotgun. "The others'll be here soon!" Mr Dawson, hidden in the undergrowth with Sergeant Phillips, felt his heartbeat racing, as he watched the ruffians scramble over the tumbled stones.

Then the Sergeant nudged him and silently pointed as another group of three burly men came running along the path towards the ruined barn. They, too, scrambled over the fallen stones and joined the others.

Another flash of lightning crackled across the sky followed by a louder, more menacing crash of thunder!

The rain began to fall heavier, and the pond, like the night before, became a bubbling cauldron!

"That's it!" whispered Sergeant Phillips, with a hint of relish in his voice.

"All six of them ready for the taking...like eggs in a chicken coop!"

He raised his left arm and twelve bright torchbeams met as a single spotlight upon the huddle of stunned, rain-soaked men!

Each of them stared, open-mouthed, into the dazzling beams, unable to move...like rabbits caught in the headlights of a car!

"Who...who's there?" called the leader, somewhat nervously.

"We'll have some fun, here!" whispered Sergeant Phillips to Mr Dawson.

In as deep a voice as he could muster, the Sergeant bellowed into the night, *"It is I...Defender of...the Creatures...of the Forest!!"*

The words echoed in the small valley, while the rain streamed down the quivering rogues' faces and another flash of lightning cracked the sky, followed by the loudest rumble of thunder yet!

"I have come...to save my beautiful deer...from your merciless hands!!
Walk from your meeting place...with your hands held high...and stand in the shallows of the pool!!"

One by one, the petrified poachers stepped gingerly from the ruins and waded obediently into the water up to their knees.

"*Leader of Coward*s...*throw your weapon of evil...into the depths of the pool*!!" echoed the Sergeant's eerie, deep tones.

In the dazzling spotlight, the shotgun looped through the air, splashed into the middle of the pool...and was gone!

But then...as circle after circle of ripples spread across the bubbling water...the most amazing thing happened which shocked and chilled the poachers, the policemen and Mr Dawson to the core!

Another ring of white lights appeared above the pool from nowhere!

Spinning faster and faster, the lights merged into a single huge halo that hovered above the treetops and then slowly began to descend!

"I can't stand no more of this!" yelled one of the ruffians in the pool.

"It's summut from Outer Space!" shrieked another.

With a wild churning of water, all six wallowed out of the haunted pool and ran back along the path as fast as their legs would carry them!

"After them, men!!" bellowed Sergeant Phillips from his hiding place.

In a flurry of arms, legs and torchbeams, the six poachers were captured and marched along the path towards the hidden police vehicles.

"I never thought I'd be so happy to see the boys in blue!" gasped one.

"I thought we'd 'ad it, right good and proper!" panted another. "You won't catch us in this forest again! That's for sure!"

"Well, I hope not!" insisted Mr Dawson. "Now, perhaps, the deer will be left alone!"

"You're welcome to 'em, mister!" mumbled the leader. "And them spinning lights! What were they anyway?"

In the pouring rain, the whole party of men stopped and took one last look back along the path. The lights had gone...vanished! All was dark and quiet except for the sound of rain falling on the trees and the undergrowth. The men walked on, leaving the pool and the ruined barn to themselves...or so they thought!

When the intruders were safely out of the way, two trotting silhouettes could be seen moving through the tree trunks towards the pool.

One was *Chandar*, the albino deer with *her* pair of riders...Jessica and Jamie. The other was the miniature mare, *Gabrielle*, with her pair of riders...Hester and Grizelda. They'd made it from the railway station!

Above them flew Nemue the nightingale, having dutifully and magically brought them all together deep in the forest.

As they made their way towards the pool, the rain eased and then stopped. There was one last flash of forked lightning and a clap of thunder that seemed to shake the trees.

Then all fell silent.

The clouds parted and drifted away, revealing the stars of the night and an almost full moon sailing across a sea of blackness.

The scene was set for magic!

In the milky moonlight, Hester and Grizelda dismounted and sat on a rock by the ruined barn. Jessica and Jamie joined them and reunited the two sisters. Hester could hardly believe how well Gwenda looked!

Jamie placed the *Ford 'T'* on the same flat mossy rock where, the night before, Queen Venetia had wished them well on their venture.

Lepho, Jonathan and Jane stepped out of the model van and waited beneath the dripping bluebells and the fern frond.

With the audience ready and *Chandar* and *Gabrielle* gently grazing among the fallen stones of the barn...the most amazing show of ancient magic was about to begin! One that had happened secretly for thousands and thousands of years back in the mists of time...

...and one that would renew the magical powers of *Aqua Crysta* for centuries to come...

Chapter 18

It was Jamie who noticed them first!

Hovering above the mirror-smooth pool, about as high as the treetops, were ten bright white globes of light forming a perfect circle!

Memories from over three centuries before flooded back into the minds of Hester and Gwenda as the circle of lights began to revolve like a carousel of white horses!

Faster and faster, and lower and lower.

Soon the globes blurred and fused into a single brilliant ring just above the pool, its brilliance doubled by its reflection in the silver water!

Then the spinning magical orbs began to slow, until they hung motionless above the pool, almost touching its surface. Broad beams of white light, one from each globe, met in the centre of their circle, where a milky, swirling mist began to form. The mist curled upwards and outwards, thickening into almost a dazzling, pure white cloud sitting on the glass of the pool!

In the heavy silence, the onlookers suddenly heard the beating of wings in the treetops. They all lifted their eyes from the cloud and saw the majestic silhouette of Merlyn the Owl circling beneath the moon and the stars!

His great wings held him aloft with no effort as he glided in a wide, sweeping circle as though he was awaiting a signal of some kind. Round and round he swept...until, at last, his sign came!

From the branch that hung over the pool came the first notes of the song of his companion, the nightingale. Her beautiful melody filled the air, silhouetted against the silence. It was what Merlyn had been waiting for...the magical message from his beloved Nemue, '*the Lady of the Lake*'. Now was the time!!

Merlyn folded his wings and fell from the sky like a stone! Down and down he fell, and his audience gasped as he vanished into the mysterious depths of the pure white cloud! At the very same moment as he disappeared, Nemue ceased her song, flew from her perch...and she, too, vanished into the swirling cloud!

The amazed onlookers hadn't long to wait before they witnessed the most wondrous miracle of magic unfold before their astonished eyes.

The cloud began to melt away and, within its wispy, remaining traces, the shape of a man began to form. A tall, white bearded man, with long, white hair and a kind face, wearing a golden gown that stretched to the water! He cast his eyes downwards and smiled a warm smile as a huge, pointed, blood-red crystal emerged from the pool, held aloft by a woman's slender, pale hand. Just the hand and arm could be seen, no more.

"I thank you, Nemue, '*Lady of the Lake*'," came the voice of Merlyn, King Arthur's timeless wizard. "I thank you for this *Crystal of Eternity*! Let me give life to its powers!"

The magician slowly reached for the crystal and took it from the hand. As he lifted it, the slender arm slipped back into the water and was gone. Merlyn raised the glowing crystal to his chest, looked lovingly at it, and then spoke the strange words of a spell.

The words were of a tongue unknown to the onlookers, until the very last ones:

"No more tomorrows, from now I say,
Forever Crystal, Forever Today!!"

The crystal in Merlyn's grasp sparkled into life, its fiery glow lighting the trees, the pool and the watching faces with flickering oranges and reds!
It was as though the forest was on fire!
Then, as the mystical crystal crackled at its brightest, the wizard lowered it into the pool and, amid a furious frenzy of sizzling and spitting, he released it back into the watery depths!
The reds and oranges vanished...and, so too, did Merlyn!
His task, and that of Nemue were done.
The magic was over!
The *Crystal of Eternity* had been reborn, its powers renewed.
The enchanted realms of *Aqua Crysta* and the *Golden Waters* were safe for centuries to come, their magic restored!

As the last traces of the magician's golden cloak faded from view, the cartwheel of beams and white globes began to spin and fuse into a single blurred disc of brilliance.
Then slowly it rose from the pool...and melted into the starry sky.
The sorcery was complete!
Tranquility and moonlight returned.

"Wowee!" gasped Jamie in the silence. "*That* was some magic show!"
"And did you see Grizelda's medallion hanging from Merlyn's neck?" burst Jessica in awe of what she had witnessed.
"It must have been Merlyn's in the first place!" came a tiny voice from the flat, mossy rock next to the pool. "Without it, he has been powerless to perform his magic for centuries. Thankyou for your help in returning it to him!"

145

Jessica and Jamie looked down curiously at the rock and were astonished to see not only their three Aqua Crystan companions...but with them were the sisters Hester and Gwenda, together with Grizelda and her faithful mare, *Gabrielle*!

But things had certainly changed!

Now *all of them* were the same diminutive Aqua Crystan size!

"But how...?" muttered Jessica in amazement. "How have you...?"

Lepho raised his arm and smiled.

"Nothing is impossible!" he said. "Merlyn's magic knows no bounds!"

"You mean Merlyn did it!" gasped Jamie. "Merlyn changed them into Aqua Crystans!!"

"And very grateful we are, too!" said Hester. "We will miss the *Golden Waters*, but we will look forward to living with our new friends in *Aqua Crysta*! I just hope that we will be welcome!"

"Of course you..." said Lepho warmly, but he was interrupted by the familiar, echoey sound of a solitary horn coming from the inlet by the mossy rock.

Small arcs of ripples appeared in the water, and then a small golden boat glided into view carrying none other than Queen Venetia herself!

"Of course you are welcome!" she announced as the little craft moored by the flat rock. "And may I thank you, Jessica and Jamie, for your endeavours. We are all, once more, in your debt. I thank you from the bottom of my heart!"

In the moonlight, everyone boarded the tiny boat and then the oarsmen guided the small craft back towards the inlet.

"Bye!" called Jonathan and Jane, waving wildly from the stern. "See you again sometime!"

Jessica and Jamie, tears in their eyes, waved back as their friends disappeared once again back into their magical realm.

"Bye!" they chorused in voices tinged with happiness and sadness, both of them wondering whether they would ever be part of the magic again.

The ripples died, silence returned and they stood by the ruined barn in the moonlight lost in the same thoughts.

After a moment or two, *Chandar* gently nudged Jamie with her nose, reminding them both that there was still one last journey to make.

"Dad!" exclaimed Jamie. "We promised we wouldn't leave *Deer Leap!*"

"Come on then, little brother, let's get going!" urged Jessica. "*Chandar* will have us back in no time!"

Jamie quickly picked up his model van, and Jessica roughly folded Gwenda's golden sheet. A second later they were ready for another dash through the trees.

As the albino deer sped through the forest leaping like a shimmering ghost over the ridges of pine needles, her two riders hung on as tightly as they could, Jessica's long, coppery hair streaming behind. Like all journeys, the return took even less time than even Jessica had expected...and, in less than no time, *Chandar* came to a halt by the front porch of the cottage.

The children dismounted, gave the deer a farewell pat...

...and then looked in horror at the front door of *Deer Leap*!

It was wide open!

"But I definitely closed it before we set off!" said Jessica. "I wouldn't leave it open for *anybody* to walk in!"

"You know what this means, don't you?" whispered Jamie, nervously looking along the hall. "Dad's got back before us!"

"He'll be furious!" whispered Jessica.

"Perhaps we'd better go for another ride on *Chandar* until he calms down!" suggested Jamie with a worried smile.

But *Chandar* had already vanished into the night!

They realised that they had no choice!

They *had* to face the music!

And the music wasn't long in coming!

And it certainly wasn't the tune they were expecting!

A strange deep voice suddenly boomed from the living-room!

A voice that certainly wasn't their father's!

"Welcome home, children of the forest. Why are you not safely tucked up in your beds on this dark, stormy night?"

Jessica and Jamie gazed at one another and froze, their hearts pounding in their chests, as two shadows moved across the living-room floor!

"Wh...who's there?" ventured Jamie, his knees turning to jelly.

There was no reply...but then a great torrent of laughter poured into the hall followed by the beaming face of Sergeant Phillips and the slightly less beaming face of Mr Dawson!

"That'll teach you two to disobey orders!" laughed Sergeant Phillips. "Your dad's been going hairless in the last couple of minutes since we got back!"

"Sorry, dad," muttered Jessica. "We were just in the gar..."

"Oh, never mind, as long as you're safe and sound!" smiled their father, giving his children a hug.

"Well," said Sergeant Phillips, "I'd best be on m' way. I daresay you won't be havin' too much bother from yon rogues for a while! I think it'll be a long time before they even go near a forest again!"

As the sound of the police-car faded down the track, Jessica, Jamie and their father headed for the kitchen.

"You know what I fancy?" beamed Mr Dawson, licking his lips. "A nice big slab of birthday cake! That's if there's any lef...!"

Just as he reached the kitchen door, he suddenly stopped and stared into the moonlit room.

All three of them stopped and stared.

For there, lying across the remains of Jamie's birthday cake was the most amazing piece of treasure you could wish to see!

It was a long dagger...almost a sword...its hilt inlaid with brilliant blue sapphires, its shaft enclosed in an ancient broad, leather sheath!

Its length was almost that of Jessica's arm and its golden handle so large that the weapon must have been wielded with two hands!

"It's the dagger lying across the crown on the medallion...and look, there's a scroll fastened to its handle!" gasped Jessica, totally mystifying her father.

"And the Eagle Owl feather's vanished!" gasped Jamie.

Jessica looked at her brother and they both looked at their poor, bewildered father.

The feather had been secretly and magically exchanged for the dagger, its beautiful jewels and polished metal shimmering and glinting in the moonlight.

"Best see what the note has to say!" Mr Dawson suggested, shaking his head and not having a clue what this latest mystery was all about!

Jessica carefully unfurled the crinkly parchment and read aloud the amazing words written in scrawly golden ink...

> ### *"Take Thee, King Arthur's Mighty Dagger, Verax,*
> ### *With Eternal Gratitude,*
> ### *Forever...Merlyn"*

Jessica and Jamie looked at one another, and then at the magnificent dagger...

...and they knew, without doubt, that the magic they had fallen into was not over yet...

...and, in their hearts, they knew it would *never* be!

After all...*"Forever Crystal,*
...Forever Merlyn,
...and above all,
...Forever Magic !!'

A ROUGH GUIDE to 'AQUA CRYSTA

Pillo

The oldest settlement in Aqua Crysta founded in Upper World year 1550 and named (1561) after Pillonius (brother of King Murgwyn) who built its first streets and market place.

Now with a population of 795 citizens, it is also the largest settlement and generally considered to be the capital of AC.

Situated beneath the magnificent Pillo Falls, the township boasts the finest crystal veins in the Kingdom. Consequently the town is full of crystal workshops where the most exquisite products are crafted.

Visit Elmwood Terrace and Vein Street in particular and you will be amazed at the craftsmanship, especially that demonstrated in the Penwort Workshop established by Augustus Penwort (who became the second mayor of Pillo in 1700, after the death of Perseus).

Pillo is famed for its bridges that span several rocky valleys which split the town into its four upland quarters known as 'Quats' (pronounced 'cats'). Try standing on the Gazing Bridge (built in 1672 by Hans Esgald) and marvel at the view of the Falls, especially when Aqua Crystan rainbows are visible. These can best be seen at 'new fall' (approx. every Upper World 2 hours) when the Falls begin the change in direction of the River Floss. They are caused by the water mists swirling against the pink crystal light. On occasions up to a dozen can be seen at once, all arching into one another. A terrific sight!

While in Pillo, absolute 'musts' to visit include:-
- the Murgwyn Museum (see the first 'Goldcrest' ship which sailed the Floss from 1581 to 1799 and the remains of the second which tragically sank in the Narrows in 1862)
- the eating and drinking establishments by the harbour, especially Calzo's (famed for its bramble wine, forget-me-not dips and chestnut gateau) Dolbetti's (for its 'Floss teas' and beech nut pies) and the Magpie Inn (for its toadstool roast with fried heather tips)
- the Ogwood's Flying Machine Memorial Park (featuring the giant model of the ill-fated invention which plunged into the Floss from almost the roof of the cavern in 1941)
- the Market Place for astounding bargains in grass-plait footwear, food delicacies and crystalware.
- the Pillo Theatre (opened 1965 and still showing Hazel Penlop's 'The Crystal Tale' plus many other productions.
- the Wimberry and Bluebell Factory (Sigmund Terrace) to witness the most mouth-watering food production processes...and to sample them!

Middle Floss

The third main settlement of with a growing population nearly 200 was first inhabite 1741. It houses the Crys who work in the Larder Ca just across the Floss and is a short walk to the cross point at the Narrows.

Perched way above the Flo the village commands sup views up and down the Fl Cavern. A visit to the Pen Cafe is a must, not only for food (supplied by the Magwi family of Torrent Lodge) but y may meet AC's playwrig Hazel Penlop, who wrote th popular 'Crystal Tale'.

Work on the first bridge acros the Floss is about to sta across the Narrows. Designe by Wilbert Snuffle of Midd Floss - the plans can b inspected at any time in th Village Hall in Penlop Square. Next door is the Fern Hat Works -well worth a visit to watch th craftmanship which turns fern fronds into fashionable headwear.

And last, but not least, and very popular with the youngsters of AC - don't forget a ride on Lightning! - the rope slide which takes you in next to no time from Penlop Square to the shores of the Floss. An experience of a life-time!

Island of Galdo

After thirty years of hollowing out, the giant stalagmite that is Galdo was finally occupied in 1580. Initially, half the population of Pillo moved to it and now the island has a population of 665.

Situated at the far southern end of the Floss Cavern from Pillo, it lies next to the Galdo Falls, but there the similarity to the older town ends.

The beautiful, soaring, tapering tower is surrounded by the vast expanse of the tranquil Lake Serentina.

On the outside, pathways spiral upwards from the harbour to the Towers of Galdo with their conical red roofs. Windows and doorways are threaded along each climbing path marking the homes of Aqua Crystans with the best views in the realm. (Travelling hint - most outer-wall families take in visitors free of charge - enquire at the Visitors Centre by the main quay, for rooms-with-a-view!)

But what makes Galdo the gem of AC is the inside of the island, entered by a tunnel beyond the 'Goldcrest' Quay.

As you walk along the passage, you will be amazed by what gradually comes into view - the hollowed out interior of the dizzyingly high, tapering cone. Just gaze upwards into the mass of swaying aerial walkways strung across from the spiralling pathways. The inner-wall houses again line the paths, this time with wonderful views up, down and across the inside of the crystal covered stalagmite.

Unlike Pillo, there are hardly any small factories and workshops. Most families work from home producing clothing, toys, games (including 'Quintz' and 'Sanctum' sets) food delicacies and carved crystal (including the George Chubb household up in the third-height famed for its crystal 'Sanctum' sets and model carvings of places in the Upper World).

All families welcome visitors to show them their skills.

The island has been the home of the King or Queen of AC since 1585 when Murgwyn moved into a new Palace - a strange term because the monarch lives in a modest home with just four rooms - but it has to be said that the crystal decor inside is staggeringly beautiful and a feast for the eyes.

(The Palace is open for visitors every so often, when the current Queen Venetia is away from home)

While in Galdo every visitor must see:-

- the Everlasting Toadstool Forest on the ground floor - it dates back to 1669 when food foraging parties into the Upper World brought spores back on the soles of their boots - it now has picnic spots, open nutshell burning fires and playground entertainments for all ages!
- the Cleff Musical Box - see all kinds of instruments being made, have a go at playing them and perhaps perform in the orchestra!
- the Towers of Galdo - added to the summit of the island in the 1750s - an absolute warren of passages and nooks and crannies, inhabited and visited by only those with a good sense for heights! Home of the famed story-teller Dandy Lopp, who eventually found sanctuary in AC after his amazing adventures in the Upper World. He still holds audiences spellbound by his stories in the Meeting Hall Cavern. (Booking required at the Visitor Centre)
- the Market Place for more bargains and idle chatter in the small cafes and bars.
- the Great Galdo Crystal Vein - just a ferry ride across Lake Serentina and you will marvel at the purple amethyst crystal prized by all crystal carvers. Join the work parties and go home with some of your hand-chiselled amethyst.

Merrick's Ledge

A tiny death-defying hamlet found at the end of a hair-raising narrow path that winds up from the Floss just south of Pillo. Only visit if you have no fear of heights! You have been warned!

If you venture there see the first home of Merrick, the third Mayor of Pillo - and oldest Aqua Crystan, and explore the fabulous labyrinth of crystal packed caves that lie behind the hamlet. You may dig out some real gems - but not too many - remember the journey down!!

Meeting Hall Cavern

Situated between Middle Floss village and Galdo, this vast cavern was opened in 1641 by King Murgwyn. Great circular banks of seats climb to its stalactite packed ceiling and on several occasions the whole population of AC has been comfortably accommodated. Concerts, public meetings and sports events take place there - most recently the first cricket match between teams from Pillo and Galdo!

map on page 51 of 'Deeper Than Yesterday'

a letter from Jessica

Hello again!

It's the day after the fantastic night before!

After all the excitement yesterday on Jamie's birthday, I've had a bit of a lie in this morning! In fact I'm writing this letter in bed with the sun shining brightly through the curtains tempting me to get up! Anyway, I can't stay in bed much longer as I've all the animals to see to.

Harry the Hedgehog, by the way, made a full recovery and we released him in March and Knapweed the Crow flew away at Easter. At the moment we've got one roe deer who was knocked down by a car, two injured herring gulls brought to us from Whitby, a young grey squirrel called 'Smudge' (who is getting up to allsorts of mischief) and a hare - another road accident - who will be ready to go in a week or two.

'Verax' the dagger is sitting on my dressing table looking fantastic in the sunlight. Poor dad just couldn't get his head round yet another mystery! His face was a picture - as were the faces of those nasty poachers last night, and that poor old ticket collector on the train!

We had a great time during the adventure, especially sailing across that wonderful lagoon and seeing all those antiques along the shore. But being in that cellar with the skeleton of Lucius was a bit scary!

It was also great to see Jonathan and Jane again and Lepho, of course. Can't wait to see them again. We must visit Aqua Crysta again and hopefully stay longer and do a bit of exploring.

But we both feel that we've got to wait for the magic to call us - we can't just 'drop in'!

Oh, nearly forgot! The 'crystalid eggs' from our Christmas adventure have changed colour. They've become dark blue and I'm sure I saw something move in one of them the other day!

Today we're going to hide 'Verax' somewhere in the forest and try and come up with some explanation for dad! It won't be easy!

Hope you have a super Summer. I'd love to hear from you - how about writing a letter?

bye for now,
love Jessica

MOONBEAM PUBLISHING
P.O. Box 100, Whitby, North Yorkshire, YO22 5WA

www.aquacrysta.com

e-mail: moonbeampublishing@yahoo.co.uk

a letter from Jamie

Hi,

It's very still in the next room! I bet my sister's fast asleep! I think I'll take advantage of the peace and quiet and write you a letter! It's the morning after our great adventure meeting Merlyn and the nasty Grizel and that great ride on the North Yorkshire Moors Steam Railway! Oh and what about that skeleton in the cupboard! What a treat that was! Wow!

It was a fantastic birthday! Can't wait for my next one! The model of the 'Clan Campbell' is already on my model shelf looking dead ace. Dad said that when he was a kid he had an electric-train set all fixed onto a big board with miles of track and loads of engines, carriages, trucks, signals and stations - and lots of model scenery and tunnels and stuff.

I think that's what I fancy next! (bet dad's keen too!!)

It was great to see Jonathan, Jane and Lepho again, especially in Jessie's bedside drawer with all the fossils and shells. Nice to see my Ford 'T' van again too! It's under my bed now, along with Tregarth's silent flute from Christmas.

Today we're going to bury 'Verax' somewhere in George - perhaps at the Dell...or we may head over to the quarry near Old Soulsyke Farm. You never know we might just catch sight of an Aqua Crystan out foraging for food! That would be a treat...but they're very hard to see!

I wonder where the wizard Merlyn and his Lady Nemue are now. It was tough luck for them being stuck as an owl and a nightingale for so long - all because of Lucius - still, at least they could fly about - that must have been ace!

If you could be another creature, what would you choose?

I think I'd be a hare (Jess is looking after one now called 'Michael' after her favourite footballer, Michael Owen).

Talking of football, our soccer team at school has had a great season beating all the other little village schools around here. We got to the final of the knockout cup and won that 3-0. I'm in midfield, but I need to run faster - perhaps that's why I want to be a hare!! Can you see a giant hare in football gear turning out for a match? Ace!

Anyway, I'm going to sneak downstairs and have a piece of birthday cake before breakfast - just to keep energy levels up for the cricket season, you understand!

Drop me a line if you want and let me know about your hobbies and favourite grub!

See you,

Jamie

a letter from Jonathan and Jane

Dear All,

We got back safe and sound from the Upper World but are already looking forward to seeing Jessica and Jamie again! Travelling in that model van wasn't much fun but it was great being at 'Deer Leap' in the drawer! We were both a bit scared when Mr Dawson came in when we were on the floor on the map, and we had to run under Jessica's bed!

He was absolutely enormous. Perhaps one day we will be able to speak to him and renew our friendship from the 1950's ...when we were all the same size!!

Hester and Gwenda are settling into Aqua Crysta happily. They have got a cosy place in Pillo on a terrace just below us, overlooking the Floss.

We don't think they're missing The Golden Waters at all. They are now the oldest people who live in Aqua Crysta, but they seem to be getting younger every time the Floss changes direction!! Grizelda is living next door to them, with Gabrielle the horse, of course. She is the one and only animal in Aqua Crysta and has already been made quite a fuss of! She has been to Galdo on the 'Goldcrest' and got a great reception .

By the way, we played a cricket match against Galdo in the Meeting Hall Cavern. It was a wonderful occasion and we intend to have many more matches. Jamie tells us that he is an 'ace batsman' so we must get him in our team next time they come here.

We're going sailing soon on Lake Serentina. Can't wait! It'll be like the Golden Waters lagoon! Write to us soon, if you have the time,

love from Jonathan and Jane

AQUA CRYSTA
Part 4

If, once again, you've been drawn into the magic of *Aqua Crysta* and would like to visit the mystical realm for a fourth time, watch out for:

'StoneSpell'

All is set for the thrilling climax of the First Series of *Aqua Crysta*.
It is Midsummer Night and ancient and rival powers battle for
magical supremacy over England.
Meet *Dodo* again, the last surviving Gargoyle; *Gargon*, the monster of the
underworld; *Spook*, the ghostly cat and *Chandar* and *Strike*, the magical deer.
Will the *crystalid eggs* hatch and can Jessica and Jamie summon the mystical
powers of *Tregarth's* silent flute and *Merlyn's* dagger, *Verax*?
Is the ancient alchemist *Lucius* really dead and who will help in the tragedy
that befalls *Deer Leap* cottage and its inhabitants?
Journey once again with the children into *Aqua Crysta* at a time
of happy celebrations and festivals...but be ready
to face the most powerful magic so far!
And be ready to witness events that mean
parts of England will *never be the same again*!!

published May 2006

*If you require signed and dedicated copies of Parts 1,2 and 3
of the First AQUA CRYSTA series and/or would like a reserved
copy of Part 4 sent to you on publication day, contact:*

MOONBEAM PUBLISHING
P.O. Box 100, Whitby, North Yorkshire, YO22 5WA
tel. 01947 811703
with details of dedications, addresses etc.
cheques only (£7.99 per book inc. p&p) payable to 'Moonbeam Publishing'